The Shadow of Death

John Paul

Copyright © 2024 by John Paul

This novel is a work of fiction. The names, characters, places, and incidents are either the product of the author's imagination or are used fictitiously. Any resemblance to actual persons, living or dead, events, or locales is entirely coincidental.

All rights reserved. No part of this book may be reproduced or used in any manner without written permission of the copyright owner except for the use of quotations in a book review.

First edition, June 2024

ISBN 979-8-218-40586-1 (paperback)
ISBN 979-8-218-40587-8 (ebook)

This book contains mature content, including graphic sexual situations, brutal violence, sexual violence, drug use, foul language, and gay-themed material.

www.iamjohnpaul.com

Chapter One

The setting sun painted the sky with a swirl of vibrant pumpkin, rich blood, and brilliant ocean among the cotton-white clouds. It had been another beautiful day in San Francisco. On the streets below, the workday was ending; the five o'clock whistle had blown for many, if only in their head. The almost silent humming of the electric buses was silenced by the loud rattling of street cars rolling along their track and the honking of cars and trucks, their drivers rushing to move in a sea of vehicles not going anywhere quickly.

The sidewalks were alive, with people walking in different directions; some talking to friends, some talking to themselves, and others staring at their phones. Still, others maneuvered through the crowd on skateboards or inline skates, sometimes barely escaping a collision with a pedestrian. It was, as always, a well-orchestrated symphony of activity and sound.

Hundreds of people, dozens of vehicles, and an endless concert of noise surrounded Jacob. He sat on the same patch of concrete almost every day, sometimes all day, leaning against the same street pole for longer than he wanted to remember. The pole that kept him upright looked to be held together with thousands of staples, which at one time were responsible for securing signs of all shapes and colors that displayed information hardly anyone ever read, except for maybe Jacob, to pass the time. People never paid attention to these signs, new or old, just as they never paid attention to Jacob.

Jacob could feel the chill of the cold pavement through his filthy jeans. Even the four pairs of stained boxers he wore under his jeans could not keep his ass warm from the cold concrete all the time. The chill he felt was often apparent in his facial expression if anyone bothered to look. Tattered like his jeans, his three shirts, torn hooded sweatshirt, and canvas jacket were riddled with holes. Looking at his hands, one would guess that Jacob had spent the last month digging in the dirt, looking for grubs and other insects to eat. His palms were slightly callused. His fingers were scratched and covered in scabs. Some of the fresher scabs had peeled back and were leaking fresh blood. His fingernails were jagged, painted with dirt, and only cut when he would bite them. His hair was sticking out from under the old CAT cap, the split ends and knots making it difficult for anyone, including Jacob, to appreciate the once natural, thick, auburn color.

For someone about to turn 19, Jacob had the face of someone ten years older. The harsh climate, the fights, and the illness picked at his slightly freckled face, evidence of the sun kissing him often as a child. The young, smiling, and loving, youthful boy of 16 could be seen in Jacob's vibrant eyes, one deep blue and the other bright green, if anyone took the time to see their sorrow and pain. Maybe he should not have run away from home, but then again, did he have any other option back then? He pondered that question as he shook the ragged paper cup. Although no one paid attention to the noise inside the cup, three pennies and a nickel danced together, almost screaming for the company of more metal.

Next to Jacob sat two backpacks. Three days ago, he stole one from a kid as he watched the small-framed boy get beat up by some bigger boys, jocks. Jacob watched as the three bigger teens beat on the smaller boy, knocking him to the ground and kicking him in the stomach and head. They were close enough that Jacob could have said something. Jacob could have yelled at them to stop. He knew he should have done something, but instead, he sat against a tree tweaked out. He was high from a few pills he scored from an older man earlier that day, his payment for a quick blow job in Golden State Park.

When the three teens grew bored of hurting the smaller boy, they left him curled up on the ground, bloody and wet. As a final punch, all three boys pulled out their dicks and pissed all over their victim. They never noticed Jacob watching, but then few ever did. Jacob saw the boy's backpack halfway between him and the boy while he lay on the ground, crying. High and confused, Jacob got up, grabbed the kid's backpack, and ran. The contents included high school-level books, old gym clothes, and a ragged gay porn magazine.

Jacob pulled the second bag off a dead body two months ago. He had been sleeping under a bridge, someplace he had called home for the past few months, when he heard shots followed by a loud thud. As he exposed his body to that cold evening, Jacob saw the dead body of a young Asian guy not far from where Jacob had been sleeping. The guy looked younger than Jacob, but he wasn't. Jacob could see the blood all over the guy's clothes and wondered how he fell over the bridge's railing. Jacob wanted to feel sadness or some emotion for the dead guy, but empathy was not a luxury for the homeless. He was more afraid of being blamed somehow. As Jacob looked at the dead body, he heard cars stop above, so he quickly took the guy's jacket, sneakers, and backpack, then ran as fast as he could.

Now, sitting on the cold pavement and angrier with the world with each passing moment, Jacob thought about the cold metal weapon in one of the bags. He never held a gun before, but he felt powerful with it by his side. The week before, alone in the park, Jacob pulled the weapon out and pretended to shoot it. It felt heavy and cold to the touch. He felt invincible as he swung the gun around. He pulled the trigger in the park, but the safety was on. That afternoon, he taught himself how to handle the gun in case he needed to protect himself one day from a violent trick or maybe a group of teen boys.

As Jacob sat against the pole now, thinking about the gun, he felt a tear roll down his face, clearing a path through his dirt-covered pores. Again, no one noticed. He was tired, exhausted with this life, and angry at everyone for keeping him stuck in this life. He could not admit he needed help; he needed to get himself out of this life. Without thinking, finally ready to release some of his rage, Jacob stood up, grabbed the Uzi from the bag, and opened fire as he spun around.

People suddenly noticed.

Jacob could hear the gears of time grinding for the first three seconds. Everything was clear, and every minute detail stood out with pin-point precision and geometrical perfection. In his mind, he was in a slow-motion movie scene; the camera focused on him, and everything around was just a blur.

Everything that followed — the pain, the confusion, the trail of death, the grief; none mattered. Jacob became intensely aware of his breathing and the smothering heat of the setting sun that draped over the scene like a freshly fallen layer of snow. A Twinkie wrapper swept up in a momentary updraft, hung beside his shoulder, reminding him that he was hungry. The sun glinted off the thousands of wrinkled facets, filling the transparent plastic with a beautifully terrible inner light—a moment of artistic beauty in the blood bath that was beginning to surround Jacob.

The bullets sprayed violently through the gun's barrel, seeming to pause and creep gently forward as the air took on a soupy, dense texture. A deadly flower blossomed before Jacob as each round added to the devastating sunburst that spread in every direction. People in comically exaggerated expressions of surprise looked around as the atmosphere thickened. Heads swiveled, trying to find the source of the chaos.

A young salesman, celebrating the closure of yet another deal, held a diet-breaking street dog and soda in his hands. He had one foot off the sidewalk, suspended mid-air as he was about to cross the street. With a tiny phone receiver tucked into his right ear, the voice inside filled him with praise for exceeding his quota. Smiling, he was oblivious to the little hand nestled in his back pocket, pulling out the wallet full of cash as a bullet penetrated his earpiece and lodged into the center of his brain. Robbed of his life and money, he fell to the ground. The young boy threw the wallet into the air, sending green paper up like confetti as bullets struck his face and hand, dead before their bodies pounded the pavement.

Two lovers strode hand in hand, matching each other step for step as they traversed the crosswalk in the opposite direction. Their perfect coordination bled from their identical jumpsuits and kicks to the twin circular O's that rounded their lips as both took bullets through their necks. A clean-shaven black man, head kinked over his shoulder so that his dreadlocks spilled majestically over the lapel of his canary yellow suit, glared at Jacob with a sneer that was two parts surprise and one part fury as two bullets painted the label of his canary suit red just before they pierced his heart.

A college freshman stooped to pick at a quarter that a prankster had epoxied to the sidewalk. His spine coiled in a tight corkscrew as he twisted to get a good look at the boy with the gun only a few feet away before two bullets drilled into his spine and a third buried into the back of his skull. Across the street, a shapely young lady in a denim skirt too short for a woman her age wore high leather fuck-me boots as she sat upon the steps that jutted forth from a building entrance. Her posture was comparatively demure; her knees were together, ankles crossed, while a spinach salad balanced tenuously on her thighs. With eyebrows plucked so that she always looked mildly surprised, they sprung up nimbly, reaching heroically for her hairline as a single bullet put a melting hole between them.

Jacob soaked up these faces and more, all oddly similar in their agonized grimaces of shock. He uttered a choked laugh through his gritted teeth as the myriad of unique personalities blurred together in the face of mortality. He wondered how many of them saw him now as clearly as he had always seen them.

Time shot forward in a frenzy of instantaneous action in the next few seconds. The bullets completed carving their decisive paths. Twisted bodies fell, each snared in its arc of descent. Meanwhile, the masses scattered, praying for a crevice, a nook, a cranny, some cover that would give reprieve to the cloud of death that engulfed the intersection. Finally, there was no sound but the short repeating clicks of the firing pin knocking against hot metal.

Shards of broken glass filled the air, sharp, clear confetti showering the violent party. Some of it danced around the streets while still more of it managed to freckle some faces of passers-by. Airbags had been deployed in many of the cars colliding; now a sea of twisted metal—art created by Jacob and placed in the middle of traffic. Blood painted the sidewalk or sprayed storefront windows, those that bullets or people had not shattered. Jacob was surprised at how quickly a new kind of chaos took over the streets.

A gas truck driven by an old Hispanic man added to the gruesome scene. In a rush to make his final delivery before he could return to the office to enjoy a planned retirement party in his honor, he sped through the traffic light as bullets started flying. One hit him in the face, almost blowing his left ear off. He shouted obscenities in his native tongue while simultaneously praying to his God. The man died almost instantly as the bullet found a new home in the center of his brain. His racing truck swerved into oncoming traffic and onto the sidewalk, running over almost a dozen people before falling into a wide staircase leading to the subway station below. The truck became a cork, stopping all foot traffic from getting in or out of the station entrance, trapping more victims.

The force of the crash pierced the gas tank, and as bullets continued to fly above ground, the gas slithered like a snake down the stairs and onto the subway platform. Within minutes, the train platform was drowning in fuel. Fumes and liquid had passengers running for shelter underground, mimicking the panic above.

The world around Jacob had frozen, and again, time stood still as if a viewer paused his TiVo to confirm a foul against his favorite ball player. At that moment, Jacob reached for one of the two remaining cartridges, reloaded his gun, grabbed his bag, and started running after sending another handful of bullets toward his audience. Jacob was the only one standing. Dozens of people were lying on the ground in pools of blood or hiding behind objects, some peaking around poles and buildings to see the aftermath. In those moments of silence that followed, Jacob ran faster than he thought he had ever run.

His heart was racing, stretching past him, trying to reach some imaginary finish line first. Jacob turned down one street and then another, never looking behind him but focused on putting distance between himself and the blood bath he had just created. Believing he had run fast enough and far enough away, he slowed down, gasping for air. Jacob held his chest tight, wanting to cry, not for what he had just done, but because of the pain he felt from running so hard, so fast. Jacob was sure he was dying. He collapsed to the ground, alone in the darkening alley.

He could hear the sirens many blocks away as police, fire, and paramedic vehicles began maneuvering through the traffic. Jacob could hear them, but he did not have the strength to move. He wondered if many people saw him leave the scene or maybe even followed him. He could not hear anyone walking near him, and the longer he sat in the alley alone, the more confident he felt about being safe from the police, for now. The moment of peace and silence was disrupted by a large blast, shaking the ground.

Emergency teams struggled to free people from the mangled metal at the intersection. Jacob had left a war zone behind. Dozens of people lay dead, and dozens more were coloring the ground red, feeling the last of their life escape them. One man who escaped all the bullets hid behind a stack of newspaper bins. Quite shaken by the incident, he pulled out a cigarette, lit it to calm himself, and threw his match away. The match, still partially lit, caught the fumes from the gas truck and landed in the pool of fuel not too far away. The street lit up with large, bright flames before a large explosion. The truck jammed in the subway entrance ignited, and the explosion sent part of the truck sailing through the air and crashing into a neighboring store window. Flames shot down the subway stairwell, setting the whole platform ablaze. Two people tried out-running the fire along the platform by jumping onto the tracks. They disappeared into the dark tunnel only to be hit by the oncoming train, unable to stop early enough to avoid the hell scene. The ball of fire above ground was massive and engulfed ten people, including the man who struck the match, now dancing flames screaming for help until they fell to the ground, charred.

Jacob was too far away to hear his victims screaming. All he heard were the explosions and the sirens. He knew he had to get up and run further away, but he did not know where he should go. He believed no place would be safe. He put the gun back in his bag and reached into his pocket, hoping to find some change, enough, he thought, to get him further away by bus. He had two pennies, some lint, and half of an old cigarette he had found on the ground earlier in the day. He got up, still shaking and weak, and walked further away from the sirens and toward the ocean. He knew it would take a couple of hours to reach the beach, but it was the only direction he believed was safe to travel.

Hours later, as workers washed the smell of death down the

city drains, the intersection was still alive with light and chatter. The police had taped off several surrounding blocks to discover what or who had caused all this chaos. Ambulances came and went, trying to clean up the dead and save as many people as possible. The police took statements from anyone conscious. Stories included the start of the chaos being road rage, someone running a red light, and even someone setting off a bomb. Everyone who offered something to the police or media correspondents had a different story. Facts were becoming harder and harder to distinguish by the time the sun finally went to bed. No one could point the finger at Jacob because no one knew him. No one could describe him. No one remembered him at all. Some recalled a boy with a gun, but they could not say whether it was a robbery they witnessed or the source of the blood bath.

By this time, Jacob was across town enjoying the distant company of high school kids having a bonfire on the beach. Jacob was not enjoying the party with them as much as he sat off in the distance, watching the dozen boys and girls run around, some laughing and others making out. Instead of being clad in bikinis and board shorts, the beach-bound kids were layered in heavy coats and thick scarves. They huddled together to keep warm from the cold Pacific air, drinking vodka and whiskey to warm their insides. Jacob longed for those days, his parent-funded joyous experiences of youth.

The kids could not see anything beyond the light generated from the pile of burning driftwood, so they did not see Jacob quietly watching them. He was angry at their perceived happiness and wanted to be a part of that life again. He wanted to smile again, to laugh. He wanted to return to that carefree life he had lived not so long ago. As he tried to remember those days, he drifted to sleep, protected from the cold with nothing more than the backpacks and an old beach blanket he found tangled against a bench. He hoped his dreams would provide peace from the chaos and death he lived through today.

Chapter Two

Nicholas stepped out of the phone store, ripping into the impossibly difficult plastic case that housed his new burner. He was excited to call Oliver, to hear his voice.

Nicholas noticed Jacob sitting on the ground when he walked into the store; he saw Jacob sitting alone in a sea of people. Jacob looked up and watched Nicholas drop a five-dollar bill into Jacob's cup. That is when Nicholas saw the beauty buried under the dirt and grime, mesmerized by Jacob's piercing, dual-colored eyes. Nicholas knew his own eyes were brilliant. He used them like the anglerfish uses its light to attract prey, and while he found Oliver's eyes stunning, seeing the mixed color vibrance of Jacob's eyes almost stopped Nicholas in his tracks. Typically, Nicholas would stop and engage, flirt with this potential prey, but today, he was on a mission. He had waited so long to talk with Oliver again, to see Oliver again, that even the bio-florescent glow of Jacob's eyes could not get Nicholas to change his course. Jacob smiled at Nicholas and thanked him for the cash.

As Nicholas pushed the door open, he noticed Jacob stand up and pull the Uzi out of his backpack. It took a few seconds for Nicholas to grasp what was happening. As the hero, Nicholas would have tackled Jacob and stopped him from painting the town red. But Nicholas was not a hero; he never claimed to be one. Instead, he watched Jacob lift the gun and start firing bullets into the crowd. Before Jacob turned around, sending bullets in every direction,

Nicholas ran back into the store and jumped over the counter for protection. He would peek around the counter when he heard the gun go quiet. Each time Nicholas looked, he could see Jacob standing, taking in what he was doing, then pulling the trigger tighter.

When the rapid-fire sound of the gun stopped for good, the sounds of screams and metal crashing into metal continued, but Nicholas decided it was safe to get out of the store. He noticed Jacob pack his bag and run. Nicholas ran after Jacob. He wanted to meet the boy who could cause so much pain and damage only to walk away. Nicholas took a few seconds to absorb the scene as he emerged from the store. The war zone was horrifically wonderful to Nicholas. Watching people trying to stop themselves or others from bleeding out was exhilarating. He wanted to take in every painful image, but he wanted to find the boy capable of such hatred even more.

Jacob knew the city well. He had lived on its streets for more than a year, so he could maneuver through the maze in a way Nicholas could not. After a few minutes of chasing Jacob, Nicholas lost him. As much as he wanted to keep looking for this strange and beautiful boy, Nicholas knew he needed to focus on getting to Oliver, so he stopped and sat on a bench. The back of the bench advertised the latest exercise fad at a discounted price. Once he slowed his breathing, Nicholas refocused on getting his phone out of the plastic once and for all so he could call Oliver.

"Hey babe," he said once Oliver answered. "I am finally in San Francisco, and I will see you in a few hours."

"Please hurry," Oliver said as he filled Nicholas in on the recent murders the sheriff had reported to Oliver.

Nicholas was perplexed by the chaos and death on the West

Coast. He chose his isolated new home in Timber Cove so he and Oliver could escape death. While Nicholas did not know Jacob, he had watched him cause chaos in the city. And, listening to Oliver regurgitate the sheriff's words, Nicholas was confident that Jacob had not killed in Timber Cover. Another murderer was causing that chaos and Nicholas knew how those murders must look to Oliver.

"I have not been there nor killed anyone in California," Nicholas responded once Oliver finished his update. Oliver wanted to question the specific reference to California but decided he did not care if Nicholas killed anyone between New York and California. He just wanted Nicholas to be home so he could hold him, hug him, and love him.

After some more banter, Nicholas hung up the phone and sat silently for a moment on the bench. The news of the deaths near Oliver had Nicholas thinking. They could be random; after all, Nicholas is not the only serial killer in the country. His thought was interrupted by sirens passing by. Nicholas looked up and watched three police cars head in the direction he had just come. He knew it was too late for those officers to do any good. Only Nicholas knew that Jacob had gotten away. Nicholas knew Jacob would remain free unless he fucked up and collided with the police on an unrelated issue and still had the gun on him, and yet Nicholas still wanted to meet this kid.

Nicholas did not know that Jacob was homeless. He never got to meet or talk with him, so as far as Nicholas knew, Jacob was somewhere safe, planning his next move: his next kill. Nicholas knew he could not sit on that bench and decipher what was happening. He needed to get to Oliver. Once he had Oliver safely in his arms, he could start to piece together the chaos of the West Coast and determine what role he could or should play in it.

Chapter Three

Two months earlier.

Juan Diego chased Xiang for longer than he thought he would have to. He was still trying to figure out how the small, framed rice muscle could easily slip out of his hands. When he put the collection of bullets through Xiang's chest, just before Xiang fell backward and over the bridge railing, Juan Diego remembered screaming at Xiang, unsure if the boy heard him.

"I loved you."

The words swam through the air, getting lost as the wind picked up. Juan Diego ran to the side of the bridge and looked down, trying to see where Xiang might have landed. He had no idea they were so high up and was confident that if the bullets had not killed Xiang, the fall did. Instead of worrying if anyone saw him and Xiang fight or heard the shots, Juan Diego searched for some steps. He needed to know if his lover survived, but more importantly, he needed to retrieve his backpack.

* * * * *

Juan Diego first saw Xiang at Club Galaxy, standing by the bar with some friends. The four boys with Xiang were taller than Xiang, but none wore a suit of muscle like him. The others were lean, too skinny for Juan Diego's taste. Juan Diego prefers men with muscle and some definition to compliment striking good looks.

Xiang had it all: a sensational smile and twinkle in his eye that captured Juan Diego almost immediately. Waiting for the bartender to serve him, Juan Diego rested his elbows on the bar and looked out onto the dance floor to the dark sea of half-naked, sweaty men gyrating to the latest dance tracks. While he was there to keep an eye on one specific individual, he was also there for anyone who looked like easy prey since he was in the mood for blood that night. He figured a loud, dark club full of drunk or drugged gay men was the perfect feeding ground. It was in other cities. As he scanned the room, Xiang smiled and stepped into Juan Diego's line of sight. The two stared at each other for longer than either meant to and before one could blink, the other was inches away.

Like most of the crowd, Xiang was shirtless, and his muscles glistened in the limited light around the bar. His flawless skin was perfectly colored and adorned with a thick, matted black hair trail running from his navel down into his low-hanging jeans. Juan Diego grabbed Xiang's body and pulled him close, gluing their bodies with sweat. Before they shared a single word Juan Diego's tongue was raping Xiang's mouth while his hands slid down into the back of Xiang's wet jeans, grabbing the plump, bare butt cheeks. Juan Diego felt Xiang get hard almost immediately. The two of them did not care about anyone around them. Some watched with jealousy, while others less attractive watched with envy. Eventually, the two came up for air. Xiang reached around Juan Diego, grabbed the drink that the bartender delivered for Juan Diego, and took a big gulp. He was parched.

"You are so fucking sexy," Xiang yelled to Juan Diego, hoping to be heard over the loud music. He could not. Juan Diego smiled, grabbed the drink from Xiang's hand, and swallowed the remaining liquid. He slammed the glass on the bar, grabbed Xiang's hand, and pulled him to a quieter corner of the club.

The two would repeat this routine at the club each Saturday night for the next few weeks. Xiang eventually gave Juan Diego his phone number, which was poorly written on a napkin. Juan Diego did not provide his, nor did he call Xiang. Juan Diego wanted Xiang to want him, so Juan Diego played this cat-and-mouse game. Xiang loved it; he loved the wild, passionate, ecstasy-laced sex the two would have in the handicapped bathroom stall each week.

Finally, three weeks after their first kiss, Juan Diego sent Xiang a text asking him to go on a date, and they skipped the club the following Saturday. Xiang's friends were annoyed that he abandoned them for a stranger. The date was a quiet dinner at a neighborhood burger bar around the corner from Xiang's apartment, followed by more sex, this time in Xiang's bed. Juan Diego knew what he was doing—he had played this game dozens of times. He would arrive in a new city, scope out the hippest gay club, and slowly seduce his next victim. Sometimes, it would take weeks to go from the first kiss to the last breath; other times, it would take months. It all depended on how much fun Juan Diego had with his prey.

Xiang was different. Juan Diego spent a few weeks scoping Xiang out before making the first move, and then he kept stringing Xiang along for weeks. Almost exactly one year after they first met, Juan Diego ended Xiang's life. Juan Diego moved slowly with Xiang, but once he had Xiang's attention, Xiang was moving fast. He hung to every word Juan Diego spat out and constantly talked about Juan Diego to his friends, even though Juan Diego and Xiang only met once a week at the club. After their fifth weekend of dancing, drinking, and having sex in the club bathroom, Xiang boldly asked Juan Diego to move in with him. He did. Xiang's friends warned Xiang against moving so quickly, but he did not listen. He was in love. Only a few of Xiang's friends saw Juan Diego in the club, but none met him. Juan Diego kept away from them because he knew they would also have to die if they got to know him.

    Before moving in with Xiang, Juan Diego bounced between his brother Pedro's apartment and a filthy motel in the Tenderloin. He preferred dumpy motels because he could come and go unnoticed. He liked the privacy, especially since he had an endless appetite for sex and death. He always rented rooms by the week and rarely brought his victims back to the motel. Instead, he would insist on returning to their home and often convince them to invite him to move in. There were four other Bay Area victims before Xiang. The CBI and FBI were working the cases, looking for a connection.

    Like Xiang, the other victims were all gay. Like Xiang, the other victims quickly became infatuated with Juan Diego, thinking about him constantly and wanting to spend more time with him than he allowed. Juan Diego lured them all in with his good looks and charm, always leaving them wanting more of him. When each victim was reported missing, their friends could not point to Juan Diego because they did not know him. He was a shadow, a stranger their friend met in the darkness of a club. Friends and family members of each victim could not provide tangible evidence to the police about where, why, or how their friend went missing. With each of the victims, they were hanging out with friends one day, and the next day, they were gone without a trace.

Eventually, each of the victims resurfaced, and all in gruesome ways. For someone who preferred to walk in the shadows, Juan Diego's murders were quite the spectacle and drastically different from each other. In addition to different ages and races, the bodies were found in different parts of the city, each killed differently—none of the typical characteristics of a serial killer. Still, then, Juan Diego was not your typical serial killer. Nicholas knew that Juan Diego was a serial killer who, like himself, preferred to mix up the profile of his victims and the way they died. For Juan Diego and Nicholas, it was more about the killing and taking of a life than about patterns for the police to identify.

Eventually, FBI Agent Calvin Dunraven was called to help with the investigations to bring calm to the city. Protests formed at the steps of the capital and throughout the city as people united to speak up about what they believed to be targeted hate crimes. In a city where being gay is celebrated, it was disconcerting for the community to live in such fear suddenly.

Xiang was already isolated from his friends by the time Juan Diego moved in, and soon after the move, Juan Diego convinced Xiang to stay in and away from his friends even more. Juan Diego even had Xiang skipping work or working remotely. He was slowly pulling Xiang away from society. And, as he did, Juan Diego demanded lots of money. The demands were not direct. Instead, they were subtle suggestions of high-dollar items to buy. Juan Diego convinced Xiang into believing he needed to buy gifts for his new boyfriend.

Xiang was the latest Silicon Valley unicorn. The software company he founded went public the month before he and Juan

Diego met, and Juan Diego had been watching Xiang for weeks prior. He knew Xiang was going to be wealthy. Juan Diego selected his victims quite purposefully. Xiang had become a billionaire overnight, and Juan Diego had plans to walk away with a lot of that money. After all, he did have a murderous lifestyle to sustain.

Xiang's friends worried about him and criticized Xiang for how mindlessly he followed and listened to his mystery boyfriend. His friends did not even know Juan Diego's name. Juan Diego had introduced himself to Xiang as Javier, taking on this brother's identity. Xiang's friends had interventions with Xiang, but none ever worked, and Xiang eventually stopped communicating with his friends and even his employees. Then, ten months after Xiang and Juan Diego first kissed, Xiang went missing. His voicemail box was full of frantic messages from friends and co-workers. His mail piled up in the lobby of his apartment building. Most of his cash had been withdrawn from his bank account. He was gone, just like the other victims, without any trace.

Juan Diego used some of Xiang's money to buy an old Victorian home far from Xiang's apartment, and as soon as the sale was final, Juan Diego lured Xiang to it under the guise of a surprise party. Once the two walked through the front door and Xiang, still blindfolded, heard the door slam closed behind him, Juan Diego turned and punched Xiang in the stomach. Xiang fell to the floor screaming, tearing the blindfold off as he dropped.

"What the fuck was that for, asshole?" Xiang yelled, looking up at Juan Diego.

"I wanted you on your knees, bitch," Juan Diego responded with an evil laugh, one Xiang had never heard before.

"If you wanted to play rough, you just had to ask," Xiang spat back, suddenly realizing the house was empty. "I thought this was supposed to be a surprise party."

"It is. Surprise," Juan Diego said as he kicked Xiang in the face with his steel-toed cowboy boot.

Xiang fell back, hitting his head on the stair railing. He screamed as he spat blood onto the floor. Juan Diego had been waiting for his night for a long time. He was going to torture Xiang in the big empty house, and he was going to enjoy it. Aside from a large oak table in the dining room, left by the previous owners, the house sat empty.

Juan Diego leaned over, grabbed Xiang by the collar, and pulled him up so he stood again. Xiang was shorter than Juan Diego, the top of his head coming up to Juan Diego's shoulder. Xiang looked at Juan Diego now with fear in his eyes and blood on his face. His head hurt. His stomach hurt. His heart was starting to hurt, too.

Juan Diego pulled Xiang in close and kissed him, forcing his tongue into Xiang's mouth, tearing at his teeth and tonsils. Xiang knew he should have been mad, but instead, he reciprocated. He knew that Juan Diego liked to play rough sometimes, but the mixed messages seemed different tonight, not as playful as before. Juan Diego stopped kissing and picked Xiang up, throwing him over his shoulder like a laundry sack. Xiang got excited. He thought the worst was behind him as Juan Diego carried Xiang into the dining room and slammed him onto the hard, cold surface of the table.

"Ouch!" Xiang yelled, trying to scold Juan Diego.

Without saying a word, Juan Diego ripped Xiang's shirt open and started kissing his smooth chest. Xiang forgot about the pain and focused on the pleasure. By the time Juan Diego had pulled Xiang's shoes and pants off, little Xiang was at full salute. Juan Diego took little Xiang in his mouth and bit hard. Xiang screamed again. Juan Diego spat him out and punched Xiang so hard in the face that he knocked Xiang out cold. With Xiang finally silent, Juan Diego admired the beautiful, little naked body before him. He enjoyed these moments when he could admire the male body in silence, but he knew it was temporary. This body would be gone soon, too.

Juan Diego picked up the syringe on the counter between the kitchen and dining room. In the needle was a cocktail of GHB and ketamine. It was enough to sedate Xiang but not kill him. After Juan Diego emptied the plastic tube into Xiang's inner thigh, he picked the small naked man up off the table and carried him into the basement, where he dropped his body into a dirty folding chair. Juan Diego cuffed Xiang's right ankle; the other end of the chain was locked around a support bean. He left Xiang sitting in the chair, his upper body leaning against the beam as Juan Diego retreated upstairs.

Hours later, Xiang woke. He was confused about how he ended up naked and chained to a pole. He still felt the sting from the punch in the face and could feel his eye swelling. His jaw hurt when he opened his mouth. He could see the teeth marks on his penis. They were turning black and blue. He yelled. He tried to pull the cuff off his ankle but could not. He looked around the windowless, dark room and wondered where he was and how he got there. Then he remembered. He remembered Juan Diego removing his clothes and remembered Juan Diego biting his penis. He yelled again, hoping someone would hear him. No one did.

For hours, Xiang yelled and struggled to get out of the cuffs.

The concrete floor felt like ice to his soles. The dampness of the basement only made Xiang colder. Being naked was not helping. Xiang walked around the limited space he could travel, looking for anything to eat or cloth himself, but primarily to help free himself from the cuffs. He was hopeful that this was part of Juan Diego's latest sadistic foreplay, but with each passing hour, he began to have much more horrible thoughts.

Juan Diego left Xiang alone in the basement for two days. On the third day, Xiang finally heard footsteps above him just as he freed himself from the cuff. He could not tell how many people were upstairs or if they could even hear him. Eventually, the basement door opened, and Juan Diego slowly descended into the dark, damp basement. On the last step, he flicked a switch to add light to the room. He could see Xiang sitting on the folding chair. He was weak, filthy, and crying for something to eat and drink.

"Why are you doing this to me?" Xiang asked, almost whispering because he barely had the strength to speak. His voice was exhausted from yelling for help. Juan Diego could see a pile of shit in a corner—the space Xiang declared his makeshift bathroom. The musty smell of the basement mixed with urine and shit revolted Juan Diego.

"Why not?" Juan Diego asked. He smiled as he looked at Xiang and was surprised when Xiang got hard.

"It looks like someone likes being a dirty pig all tied up," Juan Diego continued.

Xiang stood up, turned, and moved into a dark corner so Juan Diego could not see him. When he entered the room, Juan Diego did not notice that Xiang had finally managed to slip his foot out of the handcuff. As Juan Diego looked towards the dark corner where Xiang had retreated, he heard a noise he did not recognize, and then he saw Xiang come charging toward him with a shovel. Juan Diego pulled a gun out of his pants, and Xiang stopped in his tracks. The Uzi looked much more powerful than the shovel, and Xiang felt defeated again. Juan Diego looked around the room, taking his eyes off Xiang for a moment, and Xiang jumped forward, smacking Juan Diego with the shovel. Its rusty metal cut into Juan Diego's hand, sending the gun into the air.

Xiang swung the shovel back, hitting Juan Diego in the head and knocking him to the ground. Xiang dropped the shovel, grabbed the gun, and ran up the stairs. Once he reached the top, he slammed the door closed. Juan Diego could hear the loud clicking sound as Xiang locked the basement door. Xiang stood in the dining room naked, holding the Uzi; it was the first time he had ever held a gun. He saw his clothes still on the dining room floor, so he gathered them up and got dressed. He put the gun in the backpack he found in the dining room and ran for the front door. The house was dark. Juan Diego had all the windows painted black before he brought Xiang to the house, something Xiang had not noticed when they arrived.

As Xiang swung the front door open and looked out into the darkness of the early morning hour, he heard the basement door crash against the floor. Xiang ran, and Juan Diego followed. Xiang was still weak from hunger, but an adrenaline rush ran through him, pushing him to run as fast as he could. He did not recognize any houses, so he did not know what direction to run. Juan Diego was only a few yards behind him, and when Xiang stopped to catch his breath, Juan Diego caught up to him. The two were standing on a bridge. Far below, Jacob was restlessly sleeping. Juan Diego had other plans for Xiang, but there on the bridge, he accepted that not everything went as planned. Before Xiang could take off again, Juan Diego filled Xiang's chest with bullets.

* * * * *

When Juan Diego reached the bottom, he saw the bridge high above. He was sure that Xiang was dead. He was confident that no one could survive that fall, even without a body full of bullets. As he moved around, looking for Xiang's body, Juan Diego studied the labyrinth of homeless tents scattered under the bridge. Some were abandoned, and others had dirty, smelly people standing or sitting around campfires smoking and drinking. By the time Juan Diego found Xiang, he had been stripped of his belongings and was again naked. Juan Diego screamed.

He had secretly loved Xiang for too long. In hindsight, holding him captive might not have been the best way to show his love, Juan Diego thought as he looked at the twisted, naked body. Among the city rats, it did not take long for Xiang to be stripped of anything valuable. His dead body was left to drown in its pool of blood, food for Mother Earth.

Juan Diego still had much to learn about sharing his feelings, especially with those he claimed to love. His first real true love had been Nicholas, who was no better at showing how or if he cared. As Juan Diego looked at Xiang's bloody, naked body, he thought about Nicholas. It was time, Juan Diego thought, for he and Nicholas to reconnect—to rekindle their old flame.

Chapter Four

Nicholas met Juan Diego at camp the summer before his freshman year of high school. Resistant to any sleepaway camp, Nicholas verbally fought with Peter but ultimately lost the battle and had to spend a month at the Arizona desert camp. This camp catered to children with no siblings to help them learn to share and play nice with others. Nicholas thought the concept was ridiculous. The idea of any camp, let alone one that targeted kids like Nicholas, was the last thing he wanted to do that summer, yet it turned out to be one of the most eye-opening experiences of his youth.

A few days after Nicholas arrived at Camp Yuma, he noticed Juan Diego, who was helping set up the canoes for a group of younger boys. They had not officially met, but there was something about Juan Diego—the way he walked and held himself that had Nicholas enamored with wanting to learn more about this boy. Nicholas had only recently started finding himself attracted to boys, and he had not put a label on what or how he was feeling. Nicholas had not yet set eyes on Oliver, but when he saw Juan Diego, he immediately thought Juan Diego was the most beautiful person he had ever seen.

Juan Diego had great posture; he stood tall and confident. His brown skin was smooth and flawless, and his muscles hid impressively under his tight, second-hand clothes. His smile was intoxicating—he had perfect teeth and the fullest lips Nicholas had ever seen on anyone. But it was his eyes that captivated Nicholas.

Juan Diego could express so much emotion through his eyes. Nicholas knew the moment he saw Juan Diego — that first time when Juan Diego looked back at him, that he wanted to know Juan Diego.

As much as he wanted to talk directly to Juan Diego to learn more about the handsome brown boy busy keeping the camp in order, Nicholas did not want to show his interest. He tried to be as aloof as it appeared Juan Diego was being with him. What Nicholas did not know then was that Juan Diego had noticed Nicholas almost immediately. As all the campers arrived on the first day, Juan Diego was there to help any of the smaller ones with their luggage. Juan Diego noticed when Nicholas stepped out of the rental car wearing long pants, a hoodie, and a baseball cap, pulling a large duffle bag out behind him. He was intrigued by how different Nicholas looked compared to all the other boys in their t-shirts and shorts. Juan Diego knew at that moment that he was going to have a great summer.

* * * * *

Juan Diego looked at Nicholas like he looked at other boys — totally consumed with exploring their bodies. Each time Juan Diego tried to get close enough to Nicholas to talk with him, another boy would get to Nicholas first. Nicholas did not appreciate all the attention from the other boys. Some wanted to be his bunkmate or canoe buddy, and others wanted to be on Nicholas' team when they played sports. Nicholas was more mature, muscular, and malicious than the others and only wanted to be alone. This aloofness affected everyone he met, and all the boys wanted to be with him, be like him.

Eventually, more than a week into the month-long camp,

Juan Diego finally found Nicholas alone. Dinner had just ended, and Nicholas did not want to sit with the other boys and watch another teen comedy in the mess hall. He wanted to sit alone on the dock and enjoy the sun setting over the lake.

Juan Diego saw Nicholas leave the mess hall and so he followed him down to the lake. Before Nicholas could sit on the edge of the dock and let his bare feet splash in the cold water, Juan Diego called out to him.

"Hi," Juan Diego said, standing twenty feet behind Nicholas.

"Hi," Nicholas responded once he stopped and turned around to see Juan Diego standing at the end of the dock. He was expecting a camp counselor, not the handsome young boy he had wanted to speak with for the past week. "What do you want?"

"Can I join you?" Juan Diego asked as he walked closer to Nicholas.

"Sure," Nicholas responded.

The two boys sat side by side on the edge of the dock. They leaned back, supporting the weight of their bodies with their hands as twenty toes dangled in the cold, dark water. Nicholas' right hand touched Juan Diego's left hand as they watched the sunset. Neither moved nor acknowledged the touching hands. They sat silently until the vibrant yellow star changed the sky to orange, then red, before getting lost below the horizon. As the sun vanished, the two leaned back, lying flat on the dock, looking at the sky, searching for the stars. Their hands were no longer touching.

"It is lovely out here," Nicholas finally said, breaking the long silence. "You do not see this kind of beauty in the city."

"I don't see your kind of beauty out here much either," Juan Diego said, trying to flirt with Nicholas as he sat up and caressed Nicholas' leg.

Nicholas' whole body quivered at Juan Diego's touch. No one had touched Nicholas like that before, and he liked it; he liked how soft Juan Diego's fingers felt as they moved across his exposed skin. Nicholas was unsure what he could say; he should say that would not make him sound like an idiot, so he sat up and grabbed Juan Diego's hand from his leg and placed it on his crotch. Juan Diego could feel how excited Nicholas was, so he turned to face Nicholas and kissed him.

Nicholas pushed Juan Diego back, almost punching him.

"What the hell are you doing?" Nicholas yelled, annihilating the romantic mood that Juan Diego was trying to create.

"Kissing you," Juan Diego spat back as he jumped up, towering over Nicholas. "You put my hand on your dick, so I assumed putting my lips on your lips was not out of the question."

"I am not like that, like you," Nicholas shot back as he stood up to be more level with Juan Diego.

"What do you mean, like me?" Juan Diego asked. "You were enjoying it too, so I am unsure what suddenly changed." Juan Diego tried hiding his anger and tears as the two boys stood silently looking at each other.

Before Juan Diego could say another word, Nicholas grabbed him by the neck, pulled him close, and kissed him. Juan Diego reciprocated. After a few minutes of exchanging saliva, Nicholas pulled away and pushed Juan Diego into the lake. But, before Nicholas could run, Juan Diego grabbed Nicholas' leg, pulling

Nicholas into the lake with him. They both emerged and stood in the shallow water, completely soaked. Nicholas tried to escape, but Juan Diego pulled him close and kissed him again. Nicholas finally gave in to the seduction.

A few minutes later, Juan Diego stopped kissing Nicholas, pulled himself onto the dock, and looked back down at Nicholas.

"Next time, let's take our clothes off before getting wet," he said as he walked away, leaving Nicholas in the cold water to watch Juan Diego walk off into the darkness.

Chapter Five

Juan Diego's father was one of the many handymen who worked at the camp. Juan Diego's family could not afford to send him to any camps, so Juan Diego would work with his father, earning his own money to save and get away when he was old enough. As a first-generation Mexican American, Juan Diego Santiago knew he wanted a better life, a more prosperous life than the one he was born into, and he knew that no one was going to help him get that life—he needed to do that on his own. Juan Diego's two older sisters sometimes helped at the camp, too, but most of the time, they were working with their mother, cleaning luxury homes in and around Phoenix.

He also had two brothers who bounced between helping their mother and father work. The three of them were identical triplets. His brother Javier was not as hungry as Juan Diego for a better life. Javier enjoyed being with his family. He spent more time with his mother and sisters, often helping them clean houses. Pedro, the oldest of the three by just a few minutes, yearned for a better life, almost more so than Juan Diego. Pedro was recruited into a local gang—initiated into the street gang as a young boy, swept up by the notion of easy money as a drug runner before he was even a teenager.

The three brothers, up until their teen years, were almost inseparable. They did almost everything together. They were innocent little boys, eager to help their parents and eager to please them, too. For entertainment, the three would pretend to be each other just to see how easily they could fool people. Being identical made it easy to fool everyone, including their parents, more often than their parents appreciated.

While Juan Diego, Javier, and Pedro confided in each other about almost everything as young boys, the three shared less about their changing bodies as teenagers. Juan Diego would talk about his changing body, but the other two were not interested in listening to him. They shared a bedroom, so even though each could drown out the words, they could see the other's bodies changing constantly. It was hard to miss when you have three teenage boys growing up in a small, single room.

Javier was the most bashful and uncomfortable talking about their bodily changes. Javier was not interested in talking about boys—not like Juan Diego. He was much more interested in girls, and one girl in particular: Gabriela. They were the same age: the boys and Gabriela. They lived in the same apartment complex and attended the same church and school. Whenever he could, Javier would rush out of the apartment each morning, hoping to walk Gabriela to class. Her older brother would harass and tease Javier daily, which did not help Javier's self-esteem and confidence struggles. Gabriela's brother, Jose, was why Javier never got the nerve to ask Gabriela on a date.

Javier found it repulsive when Juan Diego and Pedro would talk about boys. He was not confident enough to say anything to his brothers, so instead, he walked out of the room or put headphones on whenever the other two talked about other boys. Javier believed that homosexuality was a sin. His brothers knew how Javier felt about the topic, so they talked about boys whenever Javier was in the room. They liked to make Javier uncomfortable every chance they got.

While they talked a lot about boys, Juan Diego never told his brothers how he liked killing boys. He would share that secret many years later, and only with Pedro. Juan Diego knew that telling Javier what he liked to do with guys would only get him in trouble. He knew Javier would share that secret with their parents and the police, ending Juan Diego's sexually deviant escapades.

Even though he was the oldest, Pedro was in the middle of the three boys regarding his sexual identity. He liked talking about boobs and penis' equally and enjoyed looking at them in magazines. He could get aroused talking with Javier about Gabriela and her girlfriends or talking with Juan Diego about any cute boy they saw on the street, especially if the boy showed some skin. While Javier and Juan Diego knew who they were and who they wanted, Pedro would spend years trying to solve that riddle for himself.

Juan Diego found any conversation about girl body parts repulsive. He never wanted to look at naked women or listen to Pedro and Javier talk about what they wanted to do with a girl. Instead, Juan Diego would tease Javier and Pedro constantly about how disgusting girls were, almost trying to force them to agree with him. He was never successful.

* * * * *

Juan Diego knew from a young age that he was different from other boys, even his brothers. He knew he liked boys, but more than that, he wanted to hurt boys. On more than one occasion, Juan Diego beat up the boys in his neighborhood. He would pretend to be one of his brothers, but when confronted, the other two would gang up and force him to confess.

At the park or school, Juan Diego would touch a boy anywhere, in any way that he could. He experienced puberty earlier than other boys, even his brothers, and had discovered how his body reacted to stimulation, and he liked it. He liked it so much that he wanted to know if other boys' bodies worked the same way. Juan Diego would lure a boy into an alley or a tool shed—anywhere he could get them alone and get them naked.

He wanted to see if they had body hair or if they had pit hair and pubic hair. He was curious about odor and whether their penis reacted to touch like his. Juan Diego would force these boys to stroke him. Sometimes, he would stroke them before beating them with a belt or stick until they bled. He liked it when the boys spewed white and red, especially red. When the boys complained to an adult, Juan Diego would appear before his jurors crying, claiming the boy violated him instead and proclaiming that what he did was an act of self-defense. He only got away with that excuse a few times.

After this scenario played out a few too many times, Juan Diego caught on to the fact that he needed to beat the boys until they stopped breathing. He realized he would stop getting in trouble if they could not tell an adult. He was a quick learner.

Juan Diego had killed two boys one year—the first year, he started to get very violent. The first had his anus torn open with a broken pitchfork handle. That boy screamed loudly and bled much more than Juan Diego expected. Juan Diego was just exploring—understanding what he could put in a boy's ass, but the power he felt as he penetrated the boy was overwhelming and exhilarating. Juan

Diego had not set out to kill the boy; he just got carried away by the excitement.

They were in a barn in a town Juan Diego had only visited once before — Juan Diego was there helping his father on a job. Juan Diego and the farmer's son, Cesar, were stacking hay in the barn when Juan Diego cornered Cesar and touched Cesar's arm. Cesar, a few years older, did not like how Juan Diego touched him, so he pushed Juan Diego away. Juan Diego retaliated with a forceful punch in the face. When blood poured out of Cesar's nose, Juan Diego half-heartedly apologized and handed Cesar a towel he found in the barn.

As Juan Diego helped Cesar stop the bleeding, he got aroused from simply touching Cesar's hands, face, and chest. Instinctively, Juan Diego pulled out his hard penis and rubbed it against Cesar's leg. Cedar freaked out and forcefully pushed Juan Diego away. Furious at being rejected, Juan Diego punched Cesar in the face again, but this time, it was with so much force that he knocked Cesar unconscious.

As Juan Diego looked at Cesar's heavyset frame lying in the hay, he decided to play with Cesar. He pulled Cesar's shorts to his ankles, flipped him on his belly, and grabbed a pitchfork he found in the barn. Juan Diego snapped the pitchfork handle over his knee, then shoved the smooth end of the broken handle into Cesar's ass. Juan Diego pushed and pulled the handle, slowly at first, tearing Cesar's ass open. Cesar woke to the pain and struggled to stop Juan Diego, but each time he tried to get up, Juan Diego would pull the handle out of Cesar and then smack him in the head with it before shoving the handle back inside Cesar. Blood was getting all over Cesar.

Juan Diego was exploring how Cesar's hole worked, but more so, he was punishing Cesar for rejecting him. Cesar tried to scream but was in too much pain to make any real noise. Angry that Cesar was not cooperating, Juan Diego grabbed the other half of the broken pitchfork and drove the spikes into the back of Cesar's neck. He pulled the pitchfork head out of Cesar's neck and momentarily basked in the red shower. Juan Diego had not intended to kill Cesar. He just wanted to explore another boy's body. He had hoped that Cesar would have been more cooperative. He had no idea that a wooden pole up the butt would be so painful, but he liked the feeling he got from watching Cesar suffer.

To cover up his first murder, Juan Diego set a match to a stack of hay in the barn and ran. Opening the barn doors, he saw Cesar's brother standing alone. He was younger—still not yet a teenager. The boy screamed when he saw the blood all over Juan Diego as he tried to flee the smoke-filled barn. Juan Diego stopped, picked the boy up, and ran back into the barn carrying the little boy. Juan Diego threw the boy on top of Cesar, and when he tried to get up, Juan Diego kicked him in the face. Juan Diego's steel toe boot crushed the little boy's face, and he lay unconscious next to his big brother—the fire ultimately consumed both.

His first two kills were unplanned and messy, but easily covered up. They set the stage for how violent Juan Diego was as a boy and how much more violent he would become as a grown man. By the time Juan Diego was 14, he had already killed five boys aged 12 to 17. Aside from Cesar's case, which was deemed an accident due to the fire, the other cases remain unsolved today.

* * * * *

It would be years before Juan Diego would share the story of Cesar with anyone, including his brothers. And the bloody path that followed for years would be one Juan Diego walked alone until he was finally ready to share his passion with Pedro.

As actively as the three discussed boy and girl body parts as they lay in bed each night talking for hours, only Juan Diego shared that he lost his virginity as a teenager. Javier was waiting until marriage; he was waiting for Gabriela. Javier was a faithful believer in God and quite religious like his mother and sisters, and he believed sex was only for married people. He enjoyed discussing sex with his brothers and looking at pictures and videos, but he remained a virgin until his wedding night, just as his faith required.

Since Pedro fell into gang life at a young age, he had to keep his sexual identity confusion a secret from anyone other than his brothers. Some of his gang members were violent and not tolerant of homosexuals. Some older gang members often harassed anyone they presumed to be gay, beating them up to within an inch of their life before pissing or spitting on them. Some even shat on their victims, then laughed with the other gang members. They were brutal and unkind people. It took a few years for Pedro to learn that gang life was not for him.

Pedro would have to watch three or four gang members hunt down a presumed gay guy and beat him up before gang-raping him. Pedro was young then and confused as to how these tough-looking, harsh-sounding, tattoo-covered, gun-toting boys who spewed testosterone and homophobia could criticize a man for being gay, hate the man for being gay, yet turn around and fuck that man in the ass as violently as they would: punishing him for presumedly being gay. Pedro found it all quite hypocritical.

By the time he was in high school, Pedro had finally been able to distance himself from gang life and completely escape that life by the time he graduated and moved away from his family, from his brothers. Pedro eventually lost his virginity in a threesome with a couple, a boy and a girl, from Berkeley University. The couple was looking to expand the boundaries of their relationship. Pedro dated them both for many months before their untimely deaths.

The three boys grew apart after high school. Javier stayed in Phoenix to help his parents and hopefully marry Gabriela one day. That never happened. Juan Diego went in search of his one true love, Nicholas, creating a bloody path of destruction in his wake. Pedro moved to San Francisco to start a new life where he would discover who he was and what truly made him happy. It was there, in Cow Hollow, that he caught up with Juan Diego years later.

Chapter Six

"I am sorry, but did you say you were looking for Nicholas?" Oliver asked Juan Diego.

"Yes," Juan Diego responded, annoyed with how Oliver was behaving.

As he studied Oliver's face, Juan Diego wondered if maybe he should quickly snap Oliver's neck now and take him out of the picture. After all, he had been waiting long enough to reunite with Nicholas and was not about to let anyone, let alone Oliver, stand in his way.

Juan Diego had been watching Oliver for a couple of years, and he was surprised that Nicholas had settled down with one person, with this person. As much as he tried over the years, Juan Diego never stopped loving Nicholas. He often thought about the summer weeks of their youth when they first met and later took a life together. He had always been a killer, much like Nicholas, but Juan Diego found that he killed more randomly when he was obsessing about Nicholas. He was focused less on who he killed and more on how he wanted to impress Nicholas.

"And how do you know Nicholas?" Oliver asked. The months leading up to this moment were confusing enough: the cloak and dagger moves, the burner phones, the isolated safe house, and now a stranger introducing himself into the plot.

"I am sorry, that sounded a little rude. But seriously, how do you know Nicholas, and more importantly, how did you know to look for him here, now?"

"Nick and I go way back," Juan Diego explained. "We went to summer camp together." He knew he was stretching the facts, but he did not care.

"Summer camp?" Oliver asked with some level of confusion in his tone. "Out here?"

"Arizona, actually," Juan Diego spat out, wishing he could have pulled that fact back. "We lost touch for several years but reconnected a few years ago. He told me he was moving to Cali, and since I live down in San Mateo, I thought I would come up and say hello and finally meet you."

"Meet me?" Oliver asked, still confused.

"Yes, sir," Juan Diego said. "Nick talked about you a lot, so I had to meet the man who made Nick so happy."

The Oliver of a few years ago would have been receptive and inviting to Juan Diego, but the new Oliver, the cynic, questioned everything coming out of Juan Diego's mouth. He had been through enough heartache and heard enough lies to find himself very well-guarded when meeting a stranger, especially one that shows up at a remote compound.

Oliver was confident that Nicholas did not tell Juan Diego about Redwood Manor. Nicholas had been too cautious about everything lately to reveal this location to someone without first telling Oliver, or so he thought.

"Well, it is nice to meet a friend of Nicholas', but I am afraid you have missed him. He is not home and will not be back until much later. If you want to leave a number, I will gladly pass it along to him for you," Oliver said, trying to remain calm and polite, even though he could feel himself becoming nervous and sweaty. Something seemed not right to him, but he could not figure it out right then, in that moment.

"Do you mind if I wait?" Juan Diego replied. It is a long drive back to San Mateo.

"I do, actually," Oliver spat back quickly. "I do not know where San Mateo is, but I do know that you cannot wait for Nicholas. It will be very late by the time he returns."

Juan Diego stepped forward, and Oliver jumped back unexpectedly. The two were staring into each other's eyes. Juan Diego saw fear, and Oliver saw darkness. Suddenly frightened, Oliver said goodbye and abruptly closed the front door. Juan Diego could hear the snap of the lock.

"Okay then," Juan Diego yelled to the door, knowing that Oliver was on the other side, afraid. "I will come back another day, Oliver. Bye for now."

Oliver looked out the window and watched Juan Diego walk down the stairs and towards the driveway. Then, Oliver realized there was no car in the driveway. He watched Juan Diego walk down the driveway and out of sight. Oliver thought it was odd that Juan Diego claimed to have come from so far yet had no car. He continued looking out the window for a little longer, worried that something terrible would happen.

Eventually, Oliver entered the kitchen and hit redial on the satellite phone. He needed to warn and inform Nicholas that a stranger might be lurking on the property.

"What's wrong?" Nicholas asked as soon as he answered the phone. Oliver could hear the sirens in the background.

"Who is Juan Diego?" Oliver almost shouted into the phone. There was silence on the other end. "And what is with all those sirens?"

"Where did you hear that name?" Nicholas fired back loudly as more police cars converged.

"From his fucking mouth when he introduced himself to me five minutes ago at the front door of the house you told me no one knew about."

Oliver was yelling. He could not control himself; he didn't want to control himself. He wanted to cry but was too focused on being mad at Nicholas. "You send me to this isolated jungle, then make me wait months alone. You are still not here, and now a total stranger, someone who says he has known about me for a long time, knocks on the front door looking for you, Nicholas Lawson."

"I am sorry, babe," Nicholas said calmly. I do not know how he found you or why he is looking for me. Juan Diego is someone from my past; I have been trying to…." His voice was muffled by the sound of an ambulance speeding by, heading towards the carnage left by Jacob.

"Where are you?" Oliver interrupted. "What is with all of the sirens?"

"I told you, I am in San Francisco. There was a mass shooting."

"Are you kidding me?"

"No," Nicholas responded. "I am a few blocks away from the chaos, trying to figure out how to get to you. I was heading to the car rental shop, but that is where the shooting occurred, not in the shop, but on the block. I am looking for other options." The lies continued.

"I cannot take any more of this, Nicholas," Oliver said through tears. "This life, your life, is just too chaotic. I cannot keep living like this. I am leaving in the morning if you are not here." Before Nicholas could speak, he heard Oliver hang up the phone.

* * * * *

When Juan Diego reached the entrance to Redwood Manor, he looked back up the drive but could no longer see the house. He liked that level of isolation. It was so typical Nick, he thought to himself as he admired the remoteness around him. Even the town seemed small and isolated. It was the perfect place to hide in plain sight. Juan Diego was confident that it would only be days before he and Nicholas would be together again. Juan Diego was delusional that Oliver was just one more object of Nicholas' desire: expendable. He had no idea how important one was to the other.

Juan Diego learned about Oliver many years ago. He remembers talking about Oliver with Nicholas while they were still in high school. Nicholas never confessed back then that he was infatuated with Oliver. Still, by the time Juan Diego caught up with Nicholas in London, it was clear to him that Nicholas was in love just from how Nicholas spoke about Oliver. That infuriated Juan Diego. He wanted Nicholas' love to be directed at him and him alone.

When Juan Diego lost track of Nicholas after their London encounter, he thought about hunting down and killing Oliver. Instead, he headed to San Francisco to see his brother, Pedro. He believed then and still believes that keeping Oliver alive would eventually help him get closer to Nicholas.

Through pure luck, Juan Diego was walking through Timber Cove a few days earlier when he saw Oliver, recognizing him almost immediately, so he assumed that Nicholas was nearby, too. Juan Diego followed Oliver back to the entrance of Redwood Manor, walking the long drive to the house and surveying it a couple of times before finally knocking on the door. He was over the moon when Oliver answered and was ecstatic at the idea that Nicholas and Oliver had come to him.

As much as Juan Diego wanted to hide out at the entrance gate to wait for Nicholas, he had no idea if or when he would show up, so he walked to the other end of Timber Cove to the motel he had called home for the last month, hiding out since killing Xiang.

When Juan Diego opened the motel room door, he could hear the water running in the shower. He closed the motel door quietly and undressed as he walked towards the bathroom, leaving a trail of clothing behind him. When he reached the bathroom, he pulled back the shower curtain and stepped into the tub.

"Me asustaste como la mierda," said Hector, the young immigrant Juan Diego picked up on the side of the highway a few days earlier. He turned towards Juan Diego and kissed him. Juan Diego returned the kiss and pushed Hector against the shower wall.

Thirty minutes later, Hector and Juan Diego lay naked in one of the two beds in the motel room. Hector was smaller than Juan Diego, shorter and skinnier. He was 18 years old and spoke very little English. Originally from Honduras, Hector, his younger brother, and his mother began the trek to America six months ago. He was alone when Juan Diego found him.

One of the cartels had killed Hector's father in a drug run that had gone wrong. His mother knew that Hector and his younger brother would not be safe and would grow up in a world of drugs and guns if they did not run away. His little brother was two years old and died of starvation in the first month of their journey. His mother fell ill on the trek from Mazatlan to Los Barilles, dying before they reached the shore. Orphaned, Hector traveled with others fleeing Honduras until they arrived in Tijuana. Once they arrived, many of them were detained, but Hector slipped through the border patrol and found himself homeless and alone in San Diego.

Juan Diego picked him up at a rest stop along Highway 1 outside Morro Bay and kept him around and alive for sex. Hector did not like how rough Juan Diego was with him, but he did enjoy the warm beds, hot meals, and the attention. Juan Diego was a hero to Hector, helping him survive in a new country. When Juan Diego spoke of freedom, money, and a job, Hector believed the lies, all promises Juan Diego had no intention of keeping. For Juan Diego, Hector was a toy to play with until he was bored, a distraction after losing Xiang.

Eventually, the two boys fell asleep in each other's arms. The only light in their seedy room was the television that had lulled them to sleep. What had started as a Mexican reality show turned into the nightly news where a pair of reporters were verbally repeating the San Francisco massacre from earlier in the day. The news station would bounce back and forth between the two reporters securely behind the news desk and video footage from the horrific scenes. Occasionally, they would get a perspective from a bystander, some covered in blood.

* * * * *

By the time Hector and Juan Diego were sound asleep on the far end of Timber Cove, Nicholas was getting out of a cab at the southern point of Timber Cove. He was exhausted and wanted nothing more than to be dropped off at the front door of Redwood Manor, but he could not run the risk of the cab driver later identifying him. He was hopeful that the lie he shared with the driver about meeting a friend in Timber Cove as they began their hike up to Oregon would be enough to ensure his privacy.

Nicholas was confident that the police back in Greenwich were growing impatient with the lack of clues Nicholas left behind when he fled their capture. He was unsure if they would start a nationwide search, but Nicholas continued taking the necessary precautions just to be safe. Once the cab was out of sight, Nicholas turned around and walked in the opposite direction, towards Redwood Manor, as he dialed Oliver's number.

"Where are you?" Oliver yelled unintentionally into the receiver.

"Believe it or not, I am walking up the drive," Nicholas said. He sounded exhausted, wiped out. "Is this really a three-mile hike?" He laughed, trying to get Oliver to laugh, too. He did not.

"Do not hang up the phone," Oliver said. "I will walk to meet you. I want to hear your voice until then. I need to know this is real." Oliver walked out the front door, down the steps, and started the long trek down the drive. He was nervous. He had not seen Nicholas in months and was not convinced that Nicholas was walking up the driveway toward him.

"Tell me about your week," Nicholas said, trying to distract Oliver. Oliver started talking about the mundane life of Redwood Manor. He found himself rambling about nothing of interest, but Nicholas was soaking it all in, loving listening to Oliver's voice.

"Stop," Nicholas said, interrupting Oliver.

"What?"

"Don't move," said Nicholas. "I see your flashlight up ahead."

"I don't have a flashlight," Oliver said, suddenly afraid that Juan Diego might still be on the driveway. "I thought that was your flashlight. I see up ahead."

"Stand still, please, Oliver. Don't get any closer to the light until I can determine who it is," Nicholas said, almost whispering now.

"Hey!" Nicholas yelled to the figure holding the flashlight. "What are you doing on my property?"

After a few seconds of silence, Nicholas heard an older man with an accent ask, "Is that you, Mr. Nicholas?"

"George?" Nicholas asked. "Is that you?"

"Si, Senor," George responded. "I mean, yes, sir, Mr. Nicholas. It is George."

Oliver heard part of the conversation through Nicholas' phone, so he continued to walk towards the light.

"What are you doing out at this late hour, George," Nicholas asked once the two men were face-to-face.

"I was doing my final round of the property, Mr. Nicholas," George said. "There have been some murders in town, so I am doing extra checks to be sure Mr. Oliver is safe until you arrive."

The two men were discussing property logistics when Oliver

reached them. George gave his flashlight to Nicholas, then pulled another out of his pocket and continued down the driveway, bidding Nicholas and Oliver a good night. Once George was out of sight, Nicholas grabbed Oliver and gave him the longest, tightest hug he could muster, given how exhausted he was. Oliver accepted the hug and the kisses that followed. He was still mad at Nicholas, but for the moment, he was happy to be back together.

Chapter Seven

The next day, Oliver woke early. Nicholas was still asleep, exhausted from his travels. Oliver wanted to stay in bed and look at Nicholas, to study his face and body, fearing that Nicholas might vanish again only too quickly. He almost forgot how Nicholas looked, tasted, and felt. Oliver never wanted to get out of bed again, but then he remembered how angry and frustrated he had been with all the games Nicholas played: how alone he had felt for the last few months. Instead of staying in bed with Nicholas, Oliver suddenly wanted to punch Nicholas, to damage the beautiful body before him. Instead, Oliver lay in bed silently, listening to Nicholas breathe. He lifted the covers and watched Nicholas' naked body expand and contract slowly, silently.

Very quickly, Oliver felt himself getting aroused. He was horny; he had been for months, and seeing Nicholas' gorgeous physique before him was not helping. He wanted to wake Nicholas and have wild, sweaty sex, but instead, he got out of bed, put on some running clothes, and began his day like he had begun dozens of days before. He went for a run.

When Nicholas woke to an empty bed, he panicked, but before he could comprehend why he was alone, Oliver walked into the bedroom, dripping in sweat. Nicholas jumped out of bed, ran over to Oliver, and grabbed him before he could escape. He did not care that Oliver was sweaty. He was happy to be with Oliver again. Oliver pulled his shirt off and kicked off his running shoes. Nicholas helped Oliver out of his running shorts and underwear and pulled him back towards the bed.

An hour later, Oliver left Nicholas in the shower. He knew that George's mother had breakfast waiting downstairs, and from his run and the sex, he was starving. He quickly got dressed and headed to the kitchen. Oliver was devouring a plate of eggs when Nicholas finally reached the kitchen.

"This is quite the spread," Nicholas said as he joined Oliver at the kitchen table.

"She does this every morning," Oliver replied. "I am not sure how I am not as big as a house, given all the food she prepares for me every day."

"This seems a little wasteful, don't you think?" Nicholas asked.

"Yes," Oliver chimed back once he swallowed. "There is more today than usual since she knows you are here. I do know that nothing goes to waste. What I do not eat either gets repurposed, or she takes it into town to one of the shelters. Or at least that is what George tells me."

As Nicholas filled his plate, Oliver started with the questions.

"Are we going to talk about Juan Diego?" Oliver asked directly.

"He was a fling from my teenage years," Nicholas said after a few minutes of awkward silence, trying to bring closure to the topic.

"Sorry, but I am not buying that load of bullshit," Oliver said, surprising himself with his bluntness and language. "That was not a teenage fling at the front door last night. That was a man on a mission, someone who has been on a mission for a long time."

"What do you mean?" Nicholas asked.

"Are you going to continue playing games with me after everything you have put me through already?" Oliver yelled. "I was not kidding last night. Either you start coming clean, or this is my last day in this fucking prison."

"He was a fling!" Nicholas yelled back defensively. "At least, that is how I choose to remember it. "We met at summer camp. He worked at the camp but not as a counselor. He was more of a handyman—kid. We connected and fooled around together in the woods. When camp ended, we agreed to stay in touch. We exchanged a few letters, but I moved on.

"The next summer, he showed up at my house. He told Peter that we were camp buddies, so Peter invited him; he even invited him to stay with us. Of course, Juan Diego took Peter up on the offer, and next thing I knew, Juan Diego was everywhere I turned."

"Did you two have sex outside of camp?" Oliver asked, not wanting an answer. He knew he should not be jealous of teenage sex, but he saw how handsome Juan Diego was, so he felt a little jealous as Nicholas told the story.

"We did," Nicholas said, happy not to lie to Oliver for a change. "And when I finally let him down, told him that we could not be boyfriends, he snapped and killed my neighbor before saying that he would keep killing people until I loved him as much he loved me."

"Hold on," Oliver interrupted. "He killed your neighbor. What did Peter do about that?"

"No one ever found out. In fact, this is the first time I have told anyone about that day. That is how much I love YOU, Oliver. I am telling you something that I have never told another living soul.

"Peter was on a business trip. Juan Diego and I were in my backyard. I do not recall what we were doing, but we saw my neighbor on her deck. She could see us. We must have been passing the ball or something. She was friendly, an older woman in her 70s. We were teenagers.

"She invited us over for some lemonade. When the three of us were in her house, Juan Diego grabbed her and said that if I did not profess my never-ending love for him right then and promised to be his boyfriend forever, he would kill her. At first, I thought he was kidding, but as soon as I told him it would be a cold day in hell before we were boyfriends, he snapped her neck right in front of me. Then he smacked her head against the marble countertop and dropped her on the floor to make it look like she slipped and hit her head."

"And you never called the police?" Oliver asked. "That is fucked up."

"He told me then that if I ever told anyone what he did, he would kill Peter and me," Nicholas said. "Then, we slipped out of her house and went back to playing in my yard as if nothing ever happened."

Nicholas did not tell Oliver that he got aroused watching Juan Diego kill his neighbor, nor that when the two boys were back in Nicholas' house, they had sex. Nicholas knew then that he was sending mixed messages to Juan Diego, and he knew now that he could not tell Oliver any of this information, certainly not if he wanted Oliver to stay in his life. While having sex with Juan Diego that afternoon all those years ago, Nicholas told Juan Diego that he was not threatened by him and that he had killed someone, too. That started a verbal battle between him and Juan Diego over who had killed more people, more violently. Juan Diego might argue that the battle continues today.

"So, at the end of that summer, he left, and I never saw him again," Nicholas lied. "I received a few letters. One time, I received a severed finger, and another time, a big toe. He even sent me a few severed dicks. One was huge.

"None of the notes with the severed body parts said who they belonged to or why he was sending them to me," Nicholas continued. "Part of me thinks it was his way of flirting or maybe threatening. I never stopped to figure any of it out." Nicholas left out the fact that he loved getting the body parts. He was turned on every time.

"I always threw the body parts into the pond off Sycamore Drive, and I burned all his letters, Nicholas continued. "I did not want any paper trail connecting me to him. He was, probably still is, a psychotic nut. You need to stay as far away from Juan Diego as possible."

Nicholas stopped talking so he could finish his breakfast before it got cold. He studied Oliver's face to see if Oliver believed the story. Nicholas surprised himself with his partially true story. Maybe, he thought, he was turning a corner in life. Maybe loving Oliver and having Oliver love him back was helping him change, helping him to be more truthful. They finished breakfast in silence.

Chapter Eight

Juan Diego sat up in bed. Hector was still lying beside him, asleep and snoring. Juan Diego looked around the room, almost reacclimating himself to the messy motel room, unsure where he was waking up. For a moment, he did not remember where he was or who the naked little boy next to him was.

His head was pounding. His vision was blurry. His latest migraine was excruciating. No amount of alcohol or other painkillers would help. He would have to suffer through it. The insufferable pain began six months ago, and fortunately, each incident lasted no more than an hour.

Juan Diego had not been to a doctor; he refused to see one. He did not trust them. His father died of a brain aneurysm many years ago quite suddenly, or at least that is how Juan Diego remembers it, and he blamed the doctors. Juan Diego did not see his father suffer for months before his brain finally ruptured, killing him almost instantly. His parents loved him enough to shield him and his siblings from the suffering his father went through. If he had seen his father's pain, then maybe Juan Diego would be taking this matter more seriously now.

Juan Diego sat in the bed, his back against the headboard, holding his head in his hands. He wished for the pain to pass quickly. This one was lasting longer than the others, he thought. He wanted to scream. Juan Diego jumped out of bed and grabbed the tequila bottle from the dresser beside the television. The bottle was almost empty. He and Hector had been drinking a lot of alcohol over the last week. Hector was much more agreeable when he was drunk. Juan Diego took a big swig of the potent clear liquid and picked up the machete beside the bottle. He admired the dried blood that painted part of the blade.

The tequila did not help subdue the pain, but it did taste good. Juan Diego walked around to the side of the bed. He pulled the sheets back where Hector lay to look at the naked boy. Juan Diego ran his hand across Hector's hairless chest and down to his unkept crotch. Hector did not wake, but his body shimmered at the touch. Juan Diego grabbed Hector's penis with his free hand, admiring how abnormally large it was for such a small, young man.

While holding the penis in one hand, Juan Diego made a clean swing with the hand holding the machete, severing Hector's head from the rest of his body and cutting right into the mattress. Still holding the limp cock, Juan Diego swung again, severing it, too. Blood poured out from Hector's neck, splattering the headboard and painting the sheets red.

Juan Diego put the limp dick in his mouth like he was going to bite on a pickle but sucked on it like a lollipop instead, enjoying the lingering taste of last night's sex. Eventually, he spit it out, and it landed in the growing pool of blood on the floor. Juan Diego turned, looked into the full-length mirror on the wall across the room, and saw his naked body covered in blood. He admired his physique and now erect penis. These kinds of killings always got Juan Diego excited.

He grabbed and relieved himself over the blood-covered body before him, then collapsed. He went limp as the pain in his head finally subsided. He was feeling better, peaceful. He fell back asleep, his body on top of Hector's as the spewing blood kept Juan Diego warm.

Chapter Nine

Jacob woke to the sounds of seagulls swarming the beach like soldiers at Normandy. They were squawking, fighting, and looking for any remnants of food. They sang and danced through the air in what looked like a rehearsed performance, occasionally dropping a bomb on their audience below.

It took Jacob a moment to realize where he was. His neck was stiff from sleeping so poorly, his head resting on the arm of the bench where he fell asleep. He could see the pile of burnt wood, remnants of the bonfire he admired from afar the night before. All the partygoers were gone, but a plethora of trash remained for the seagulls to enjoy.

Couples were walking the beach, enjoying the serenity of a sunrise stroll. A few older men were walking alone with headphones over their ears, watching lights on their metal detectors, hoping to strike it rich; none ever did. Some younger people were running. Jacob was amazed at how alive the beach was at this early hour. He sat up and opened the backpacks to check if the gun was still inside. Jacob was suddenly aware of what he had done the day before. Visions of the chaos sped through his mind as he tried to understand what he did and why he did it. He knew that the police would be looking for him, assuming they could figure out that he was responsible for the death and destruction. He knew the authorities would be looking everywhere for a suspect.

Yesterday, Jacob had not stopped to think about whether his actions were captured on security cameras or cell phones. He had not thought about what he was doing then, what he had done. At the time, he was being reactionary, not thinking about the consequences or the death. He was releasing his pain. Sitting on the bench crying, Jacob wished he could go back in time. He told himself that if he could, he never would have pulled out the gun and probably would have taken the gun from the dead Asian kid, either. He wanted to get rid of it now, but he felt too many people were on the beach. Jacob was confident someone would see him drop the gun in the sand or a trashcan and call the police. If he escaped cameras yesterday, he might not be lucky enough to escape the eyes of an onlooker today.

Jacob sat up on the bench, quietly crying for longer than he wanted, reliving the nightmare of the day before. While sitting in the serene space of the warm rising sun and the soothing sound of ocean waves crashing along the shore, Jacob decided that he was going to get his life together. It was time for his yearlong pity party to come to an end. He was tired of being a homeless mess, tired of having sex for money, tired of living this life. Jacob wanted to return to the life he once had, to be clean again, and maybe even return to Greenwich, so he gathered his bags and headed to the bathhouse a few yards away to pee and wash up.

Jacob emerged from the bathhouse cleaner than he had been in a long time. While it was hard to bathe in the old, broken sink, he had managed to wash his entire body. He was thankful that no one walked into the bathhouse while he was getting clean.

He had stripped out of all his clothes, stood naked in front of the small graffiti-covered mirror, and scrubbed his entire body with what little soap he could squirt out of the bottles next to each sink. Jacob was determined to change. Once he felt clean, he stood beside the air blower to dry his whole body. The heat felt comforting. The warm air was arousing. Fully erect, he wished the bathroom door had a lock but was glad no one had walked in. Once completely limp and dry, Jacob pulled some clothes from one of the stolen backpacks.

Fortunately for him, the high school boy was almost the same size, so his newer, cleaner clothes fit well and felt good, soft against his skin. They were gym clothes: shorts and a T-shirt, but Jacob did not mind. They were cleaner than anything he had worn in months.

Jacob walked into the bathhouse as a filthy, smelly homeless kid and walked out looking like a new man, feeling like a new man. He left his old clothes in the bathhouse in an overflowing trash can. He contemplated dropping the gun in the same trashcan since he was alone but decided to hold on to it for a little longer. He did not want to leave it and his clothes together in case someone found them and could somehow identify him. He had watched enough crime TV when he was younger to believe anything was possible.

Although clean, Jacob still had no money and needed a proper shower and deodorant, but he felt cleaner; he looked cleaner. He pulled his hair back and tied it with a rubber band he found in the backpack, forming a small man bun on his head. He felt this helped him look less homeless and more bohemian. Refreshed, Jacob walked off the beach and back toward the homeless camp he called home for the last few months.

Police cars whizzed by Jacob, each time making him jump, thinking they had already solved the case and were coming for him. Eventually, he returned to the homeless camp, but as he got close, he noticed more police cars. It had been weeks since he saw the dead Asian boy, since Xiang fell to his death, thanks to Juan Diego. Jacob assumed the dead body was discovered weeks ago when he heard sirens that night. He had not stuck around to find out and had not been back since. He could not imagine what the police could be doing at the homeless camp now. Jacob got as close as possible, joining a growing crowd of onlookers and protestors.

"What is going on?" he asked a tall, skinny boy holding a skateboard.

"The fucking pigs are raiding the homeless camp under the bridge. They have been here for hours. They are messing with everyone, dude."

"Why?" Jacob asked.

"Who knows, man," the kid replied. "It's what they do, you know. They beat up the little guy."

While Jacob sat on the sidewalk watching the police put some homeless campers into a police van and the city workers throw the homeless campers' possessions into a trash truck, he wondered how he got trapped in that life and asked himself if he would still have fallen into it if had stayed with Pedro. Either way, Jacob was excited about his decision to change, to get better. As he sat watching, waiting, he was unaware of Juan Diego watching him.

* * * * *

Juan Diego was startled awake by the horn of a semi-truck outside his motel room. He sprung up, realizing he was matted to Hector, almost glued together with blood. He peeled himself from Hector, admiring the chaos. His head felt so much better—he was a new man. As he got out of bed, he stepped on the severed penis sitting in a pool of dried blood. Juan Diego almost lost his balance. He looked down and laughed at the site of the large, uncut brown log.

The room was a disaster. Blood was everywhere. Juan Diego kicked the penis under the bed and walked towards the bathroom. He needed a hot shower. After spending much longer submerged in the hot waterfall than planned, Juan Diego emerged from the bathroom feeling cleaner and fresher. He grabbed some clothes out of a duffle bag and got dressed.

The television was still on; it had been on all night, and the news station was still reporting on the massacre from the day before. There were still no images of Jacob, but plenty of the devastation he left behind. A reporter talked about the gun used in the attack. The police could already say with certainty that they knew the events began with a single gunman as they described the pile of shells on the ground by the pole where Jacob always sat. Juan Diego listened to the reporter and believed that his gun, the one Xiang stole, was the weapon the police were describing.

"Fuck!" Juan Diego yelled, frustrated that his plan continued to unravel. "I fucking hate you, Xiang. You fucked everything up. Why did you have to run?" Juan Diego knew Xiang could not hear him, but he was angry, frustrated that he now had to figure out where that gun was before he could get back to confronting Oliver and Nicholas. His fingerprints were on that gun, and the last thing Juan Diego needed was for it to end up in the hands of the police.

When Juan Diego got to the homeless camp the night Xiang died, he did not find the gun. He looked everywhere, but Xiang had already been stripped of anything of value. Juan Diego tormented several homeless people that night, asking for any information about the gun and the bag that Xiang had as he landed on the ground. Three homeless people died that night as Juan Diego stabbed or smashed their heads into the ground because they did not help him. More would have been killed if the police had not arrived as quickly as they had that night. Juan Diego escaped but with no information about the whereabouts of his gun or his bag.

As he watched the news now, Juan Diego decided to return to where Xiang died to see if he could find the person who had his gun. He was convinced that the person who stole the gun was homeless, and he hoped they would return to the camp, believing it was safe now. Juan Diego walked out of the motel room, putting the "Do not disturb" sign on the outside door handle as he closed the door behind him. He did not want anyone to find Hector just yet.

Juan Diego broke into a car in the motel parking lot and sped south toward San Francisco. He knew that the car would be reported stolen soon, so he drove fast. Once he crossed the Golden Gate Bridge, he parked the car along the marina and walked away. He knew walking to where he killed Xiang would take a long time, but he did not want to leave the stolen car close to the murder scene for fear that the police would make some connection between the two. Juan Diego was overly cautious about his killings lately, thoroughly covering all his tracks.

As he walked through San Francisco, Juan Diego thought about Nicholas. He thought about Oliver. His plan to be with Nicholas was not working out very well. He wondered if he was getting sloppy or maybe his love was blinding him from his mission.

He thought about Xiang and how much he did love Xiang—not as much as he loved Nicholas, but still more than he had loved anyone else in a long time. He wondered if he could love anyone else as much as he loved Nicholas while at the same time trying to remember why he loved Nicholas so much.

Juan Diego was confident that if he could sit down with Nicholas, he could make him see how much he loved him, how much they loved each other. He was convinced that Nicholas still loved him as much as he loved Nicholas. Their time in London made that clear to him.

As he walked over the hills of San Francisco, taking in the city's beauty, Juan Diego started to cry. He could feel another headache coming on. They were coming more frequently, and he knew he needed to let Nicholas know he was dying; he needed Nicholas to love him again before he died.

He popped into a convenience store and bought some aspirin and alcohol to kill his headache temporarily. While in line to check out, he saw a boy walk past the store carrying his backpack. That image slapped Juan Diego in the face. He knew that his death and his love for Nicholas had to wait. He needed to get that bag back. Aside from some clothes, it included mementos of Nicholas that he had acquired over the years, but more importantly, it contained a journal of his tracking Nicholas and Oliver. That one piece of evidence could come back to bite him if his master plan did not execute as it had been laid out. So far, the plan was riddled with holes.

Chapter Ten

Juan Diego headed in the same direction as the boy with his bag. They walked much farther than Juan Diego wanted, but eventually, Juan Diego caught up to the boy only to find they had walked into the middle of a protest. Juan Diego stood across the street from the boy, leaning against a light pole, trying to understand what was happening. He blended in with the dozens of other onlookers, watching the police violate the rights of the homeless.

Protestors marched in circles with handmade signs condemning the police for their brutal behavior toward the homeless camp and its temporary residents. Some people were blowing whistles while others chanted. The scene was loud but calm and controlled. The situation had not yet warranted any news vans, but Juan Diego could see it escalating to that point soon, so he knew he needed to act quickly. He did not want to be on television.

When Juan Diego looked across the street, he noticed the two backpacks sitting on the ground in front of the boy. Juan Diego had no interest in the smaller bag, but he knew immediately that the bigger bag was his. When Jacob looked up, he saw Juan Diego staring at him.

Jacob smiled.

It had been many months since Jacob last saw Pedro.

* * * * *

Pedro was the first person Jacob met in San Francisco. When Jacob stepped off the bus, he was excited to explore a new city, to be free from the conservative prison of home. In all his excitement, Jacob mindlessly walked out of the bus station, only to collide with Pedro.

Jacob took the brunt of the collision, scraping his knees and elbows. People walked around the two men entangled on the ground, ignoring them. Pedro, who had fallen on top of Jacob, suffered no physical injury but was embarrassed.

"I am so sorry," Pedro said to Jacob as if Pedro was the reason for their pile-up.

"It's okay," Jacob said. "It was totally my fault. I was not watching where I was going. I am just so excited to finally be in San Francisco."

Pedro stood up and then reached his hand out to help Jacob stand.

"Oh no, you are bleeding," Pedro said, pulling Jacob over to a bench. "Sit here."

Jacob sat on the bench and watched as Pedro pulled a handkerchief out of his back pocket and a bottle of water from his backpack. Pedro poured water on the cloth before gently applying it to Jacob's wounds. It stung. Jacob let out a small yelp, trying not to look like a teenager in need of his mother.

"Sorry if that hurts," Pedro said. "But we need to get that cleaned up. Those cuts look deep."

"It's okay," said Jacob. "Thank you for helping me."

Jacob wanted to say more, but he was in pain. His right elbow was scraped, and the fall had torn a hole in his long-sleeve shirt, but the more significant issue was with his knees. He wore shorts, so both knees were torn open when the exposed skin kissed the dirty concrete.

After a few minutes, thanks to Pedro's help, the bleeding stopped. Jacob had blood on his shorts, and some dried blood still streaked down his legs while Pedro's once white handkerchief was soaking in blood and water.

"You need to get these bandaged up," Pedro said. "Do you live around here?"

"No," Jacob replied. "I just arrived; I just got off the bus. I am not sure where I am going to go yet."

Jacob looked at Pedro and smiled.

Pedro looked into Jacob's eyes and could see that he was hurt; almost terrified now that he was alone in a new city, but Pedro could hear the excitement and wonder in Jacob's voice. He had been in Jacob's shoes before. He knew what it felt like to arrive in a new city, not knowing anyone but excited at what could be possible.

"My name is Pedro," he finally said as he extended his hand.

"Jacob," Jacob responded. "Thank you again. It is nice to meet you."

"It is nice to meet you, too," Pedro said. "Come with me. I have bandages at home. I do not live too far. It is the least I can do. Can you walk?"

While hesitant to go home with a stranger so quickly after arriving in a new city, Jacob stood up and decided that Pedro was a good person, so he walked with Pedro for five blocks along the waterfront before turning and climbing a steep hill. Jacob was fascinated with how the sidewalk had steps built into it. Eventually, they stopped in front of a small apartment building. Thanks to all the walking, Jacob was bleeding again.

"This is it," Pedro said with pride. "And good thing. Look at all that fresh blood."

Inside, Jacob carefully sat on a chair, making sure not to get blood on his new friend's furniture. He sat alone for longer than he wanted but could hear Pedro making noises in the other room, looking for supplies to bandage Jacob.

"You have a nice place," Jacob yelled, trying to fill the air with conversation.

"Thanks," Pedro yelled back.

"Do you live alone?" Jacob asked. "He looked around the studio apartment in awe. He had never seen such a small living space before.

"Yes," Pedro said, returning to the living room with a first-aid kit. "It is small, but it is all mine."

Pedro smiled as he returned to playing doctor for Jacob. He rewashed both knees, this time with rubbing alcohol, before applying bandages. Jacob screamed and was instantly embarrassed at his childish behavior.

"Sorry," Jacob said, trying to act older than he was.

"Don't be silly," Pedro said. "I know it hurts, but this will get all that dirt out and help you heal faster."

As Pedro finished putting a bandage on each knee, he unconsciously kissed Jacob's knees. When he was a child, Pedro's mother kissed his cuts as she bandaged them, so he instinctively did the same to Jacob.

"Sorry if that was weird," Pedro said as he realized what he had done. "My mother always did that. It did not do anything medically, but it always made us feel better."

"It was not weird," Jacob said. "It was quite nice."

"Do you want to shower and put on some clothes not covered in blood," Pedro asked. "The bathroom is around the corner."

Jacob declined the offer, and the two sat and talked instead.

The conversation took a few minutes to get going when they no longer had the accident and injury to talk about. Still, Jacob eventually told Pedro about running away, about wanting a new life, and how he thought San Francisco was the place for his new beginning and lifestyle.

Pedro listened. He had once been a young kid in a strange city, and he remembered the first people he met and how welcomed they made him feel. He wanted to do the same for Jacob. The two talked for hours, and before they knew it, Pedro turned on some lights and asked Jacob if he wanted to stay for dinner. Jacob welcomed the offer for food. Pedro made veggie quesadillas for them, which they enjoyed with some tequila.

By the end of the first glass, Jacob was tipsy and tired. He had only tasted beer before, stealing sips from his father's bottle when he was not looking. Actual alcohol had not passed through his lips until today, and he was feeling its effects quickly.

"I am sorry," Jacob said, realizing he had apologized a lot to Pedro. "That drink is strong."

"I take it you have not had tequila before," Pedro said, laughing. "How old are you?"

Jacob thought about lying about his age, but he liked Pedro and how comfortable he made his first day in a new city feel, so he told Pedro the truth. Jacob expected Pedro to get mad or call the police, but instead, he stood up, walked over to Jacob, and hugged him.

"Dude," started Pedro. "I get it. I was in your shoes once. It would be best if you slept here tonight. Before you are too drunk, take a shower. I will get some blankets for you."

Jacob agreed with Pedro and took a long, hot shower. When Jacob emerged from the bathroom, he realized how tired, and how drunk he really was. Pedro had already pulled the Murphy bed out of the wall and cleaned up dinner. They were both ready for sleep.

The following day, Jacob woke with a slight hangover but well rested. He saw Pedro silently sleeping next to him in the bed that took up most of what was a living room the night before. Jacob sat up in bed and watched Pedro sleep. He looked peaceful. The room felt welcoming and safer than it did last night. Jacob started to quietly cry.

* * * * *

Neither Jacob nor Juan Diego moved when they saw each other. They each watched the other, ignoring everyone and everything around them. Juan Diego shook his head, indicating to Jacob to move. Then Juan Diego took a few steps to his right. Jacob stood up, grabbed both bags and moved to his left. They continued to play this silent game until they were a few dozen feet away from the bridge, farther from the commotion and the police. But they were still on opposite sides of the street. Juan Diego finally waved. Jacob waved back and then crossed the street.

"Hi," Jacob said.

"Hey," said Juan Diego.

"It is so great to see you again," Jacob sang as he put his bags down so he could hug Juan Diego.

Juan Diego was confused by Jacob's behavior, but he accepted the hug and reciprocated. Jacob held on to Juan Diego tightly and for longer than Juan Diego wanted.

"Are you okay?" Juan Diego asked.

"Yes," Jacob replied. "It is just so nice to see a friend."

Jacob finally loosened his grip on Juan Diego and stepped back.

"You look fantastic," Jacob said. "Taller. Leaner."

"Thanks," Juan Diego responded, still confused.

"What are you doing here?"

At that moment, Juan Diego realized what was happening. A few months earlier, he said goodbye to his brother, Pedro, as he boarded a bus for New York. Juan Diego knew that Pedro had been living in San Francisco for some time prior and suddenly realized that the boy before him—Jacob, must have been a friend or trick of Pedro's. He knew now that seducing Jacob to get what he wanted would be easier than he initially thought.

"Looking for you, of course," Juan Diego lied.

"You remember me?" Jacob asked, blushing. "That is so awesome."

"How could I forget such an adorable face?" Juan Diego asked as he cupped Jacob's face in his hand.

"I am sorry that I slipped out of your apartment before you woke that morning, Pedro," Jacob apologized. "You had been so kind to me, and I was crushing on you. Not saying goodbye seemed easier."

"It's okay, kid," Juan Diego said. He just wanted his backpack so he could get back to tracking Oliver and Nicholas.

"Seriously, man," Jacob continued. "No one has let me crash with them like you did that first day I arrived. Sneaking out while you were sleeping was one of my biggest mistakes. I know that now. I am just glad I ran into you so I could apologize."

"It's all good, man," Juan Diego said.

"You want to get out of here?" Juan Diego finally asked quite aggressively as he softly touched Jacob's stomach.

Jacob was used to propositions like this one. Since walking out on Pedro, he had accidentally become quite good at turning tricks to make money. He was a good-looking guy, and he knew it. Pedro had not propositioned Jacob the night he spent with him. He treated Jacob like a little brother in need, so suggesting they get frisky now seemed a little out of character for Pedro, thought Jacob. Still, Jacob was horny, attracted to Pedro, and felt like this would finally be a way to truly show his appreciation to Pedro.

"Yeah, man," Jacob replied. "What did you have in mind?"

"Here, let me help you with those," Juan Diego said as he grabbed his backpack from Jacob. While resistant at first, Jacob let go of the bag, and as soon as Juan Diego hooked it over his shoulder, Jacob grabbed Juan Diego's free hand. They walked a few blocks, hand in hand, toward the park.

Jacob liked the way Juan Diego's hand felt. It was bigger, almost swallowing Jacob's hand. He did not remember Pedro's hands being so strong. It comforted Jacob; it reminded him of when his father would hold his hand to cross the street when he was younger. Thinking of his father at that moment, Jacob remembered that he was going to clean up his life—get back to his father and his family. He was telling himself this would be his last trick.

Once they reached the park, they walked to an overgrown and unkept section and into some brush. Once the brush hid them, Jacob dropped his backpack, pulled the other off Juan Diego's shoulder, and tried to kiss him.

"So, what do you want to do?" Jacob asked.

Juan Diego pushed Jacob back, knocking him to the ground.

"What the fuck, dude!" Jacob yelled as he lay on the ground.

Juan Diego did not say anything. He looked down at the scared, privileged white boy and wondered about his backstory. Juan Diego did not know Jacob; he had never seen him before today, but he could look at him and know that while he might be homeless or lost now, that was not always the case. Rich people need so much affirmation, he thought; so much attention that they often appear desperate without even realizing it. Xiang did, remembered Juan Diego as he looked down at Jacob.

"You are pathetic," Juan Diego spat to Jacob. "I bet you had a wonderful life before you threw it all away to be the sad, self-absorbed prick you are now. Or maybe you always were that prick, and your parents finally put you in your place."

"I said I was sorry, Pedro," Jacob said. "What happened to you? You were so kind to me a year ago. Are you really this mad that I walked out on you without saying goodbye?"

"I am not Pedro!" Juan Diego yelled. "You stole something that belongs to me, and I am here to take it back."

"Not Pedro?" Jacob asked, confused.

Chapter Eleven

"Pedro is my brother," Juan Diego yelled. "There are three of us, all identical, although I am the most handsome one."

Jacob looked up at Juan Diego, studying his face. He could not believe how much Juan Diego looked exactly like Pedro.

"Well, you are certainly the more aggressive one," Jacob said. "Your brother was very kind to me. He never treated me like you are treating me now."

Juan Diego laughed as he picked up his backpack, unzipped it, and saw the Uzi inside. Jacob tried to stand up, but Juan Diego pulled the gun out of the bag and pointed it at him.

"It looks like someone has been busy," Juan Diego commented. "It is YOU they are talking about on the news. You are the little fuck who stole my gun and lit up the streets. Kudos. It takes guts to massacre a city block at rush hour."

"Take the gun and the bag. Just leave me alone, please," Jacob pleaded, still on the ground, looking up at Juan Diego. "I am sorry I took your bag. I found it on a dead guy. How was I supposed to know it belonged to you?"

"That little prick stole it from me just before I killed him," Juan Diego said as he remembered the night his plan started unraveling.

Juan Diego had not intended to confess to killing Xiang so quickly or easily. He looked back into the bag and found his journals, thrilled that Jacob had not thrown them away or damaged them. He pulled them out and let the bag drop to the ground.

"Did you read these?" he asked, acting like a teen girl accusing her mother of reading her diary.

"No, man. I did not even know those were in there," Jacob lied through tears. "I don't know how you might be related to the Asian kid, but please just let me go. I will not say anything to anyone."

"Oh, I am not worried about you going to the police," Juan Diego spat. "You are a wanted man. Killing you now would be doing them a favor."

Jacob had read every page of Juan Diego's journals. He was fascinated with the stories. When he read them weeks ago while sitting against the streetlight pole, hoping for someone to notice him and give him some coin, he thought the author was psychotic. He could not tell if the journals were confessions, an agenda, or just the fantastical writings of someone, but he enjoyed every page, every word. He had mixed feelings now, excited to have met the author but afraid that he was about to become the next story in the journal.

When Jacob read the journals, he believed that some of the places described sounded oddly like Greenwich, and the more he reread the words, he concluded that he might even know the 'Oliver' character. Jacob's older brother went to school with a kid named Oliver. Jacob could not recall Oliver's last name, but he remembered seeing Oliver hang out with his brother now and again when Oliver would tutor him. Jacob would make it a point to be home when his brother got tutored. Jacob was smitten with Oliver. He was one of the first boys Jacob crushed on.

"Please do not kill me," Jacob pleaded. "One killer to another, have some mercy."

"Killer?" asked Juan Diego. "You did read my journals, you little prick, didn't you?"

Jacob thought about sticking to his lie, but he also thought about how admitting the truth might help him, especially if he mentioned Oliver.

"Where are you from?" Juan Diego asked. "And what is your name?"

"My name is Jacob, and I am from Greenwich, Connecticut."

"No fucking way!" Juan Diego spoke softly now as if they were becoming buddies. "How long have you been in San Francisco?"

Juan Diego laughed to himself. Five minutes earlier, he thought he was going to kill Jacob, but now he wondered if Jacob could be a connection to Oliver or Nicholas. Greenwich was not that big of a city, Juan Diego thought.

"Why do you care?" Jacob asked. "You are just going to kill me, aren't you? Go ahead. I deserve it after what I did yesterday."

"Do you know Oliver McPherson?" Juan Diego asked. He was doubtful of the answer, but given his current fascination with Oliver and his continued love for Nicholas, he had to ask, especially since Jacob claimed to be from Greenwich.

Jacob thought about the question for longer than Juan Diego wanted the silence to surround them.

"Does he have blonde hair and intoxicatingly beautiful blue eyes?"

"Yes," Juan Diego said with a smile as he thought about the other day when he was eye to eye with Oliver.

"Then I believe I do," Jacob said, knowing all too well that he knew Oliver. He still crushed on him even after all these years. "If we are talking about the same guy, he tutored my brother in high school. It's been a minute since I last saw him, but I know him. Do you know him, too? Jacob knew that Juan Diego knew Oliver or knew of him. Oliver was one of the main characters in the journals.

"Yes, I know him, and right now, he is trying to steal my boyfriend," Juan Diego said. "I ran into him yesterday, and I think it is time for him to die."

"Hopefully, you do not think it is my time to die," Jacob said, laughing to lighten the mood. "Maybe we can help each other out."

"How can you possibly help me?" Juan Diego asked, still waving the gun, reminding Jacob of who was in charge.

"Well, for starters," Jacob said. "I can talk with Oliver. He will remember me, for sure. I can distract him enough so you can get your boyfriend back. I am not sure he needs to die for stealing your boyfriend, right?"

"You don't even know me," Juan Diego said. "And I am holding you at gunpoint in a bush. Why would you want to help me?"

"Well, you might not be Pedro," Jacob started. "But he helped me when I needed it most, so it is only fitting that I can help his brother in a moment of need.

"It's a win-win."

"How do you figure?" Juan Diego asked.

"Full disclosure," Jacob said. "I crushed on Oliver for years. I want to date him if he is still as handsome as he was in high school. You get your man, and I get mine. Win-win."

Jacob knew that he was not going to date Oliver. He doubted Oliver would remember him, let alone his brother. He was saying whatever he thought Juan Diego wanted to hear. He did not want to be killed. Jacob knew the minute Juan Diego knocked him to the ground, he would never see his family again. He was surprised that he could distract Juan Diego for as long as he had thus far.

"That makes some sense," Juan Diego said.

Juan Diego put the journals and gun back in the backpack and then reached out his hand to help Jacob stand up. They stood within inches of each other. Jacob had to look up to see into Juan Diego's eyes. Juan Diego looked down and noticed the two different-colored eyes for the first time since they started talking. The blue was as bright as Oliver's, and the green was as vibrant as Nicholas's. Juan Diego could not believe it. He was temporarily lost in Jacob's eyes before shaking himself back to reality.

"Before we go," Juan Diego started. "Let's have some fun. Take your clothes off."

Jacob was not about to get naked in the park. He had turned enough tricks here to know that people were always watching. He needed to be able to run away fast if ever caught.

"No," said Jacob. "This is not the place to get naked. We will get caught, and I know neither of us wants to sit in a police station anytime soon."

"Come on," Juan Diego continued. "You know you want a piece of this," pointing to himself. "I will even let you decide which position you want," Juan Diego lied. "I am excited that you know Oliver. You are my hero. You are going to save my relationship."

Juan Diego knew how to make his victims feel like they were

on top of the world, in charge. His charm was intoxicating. He had no intention of having sex with Jacob or even letting him emerge from this isolated area of the park, but as with most of his victims, Juan Diego was baiting Jacob for the kill.

Reluctantly, Jacob removed his gym clothes and stood completely naked before Juan Diego. He suddenly felt violated, ashamed of what he thought he was about to do. He cupped his crotch as Juan Diego admired the boy before him.

"What are you being bashful about?" Juan Diego asked. "You have a sexy body. I bet every pathetic married or lonely pervert in town is excited when they find you on the corner."

Jacob started to feel more comfortable. Juan Diego was saying all the right things to get Jacob to lower his guard and trust that Juan Diego was being authentic. Jacob uncupped his crotch and confidently took two steps forward to be within inches of Juan Diego again. Jacob gently grabbed Juan Diego's jeans with one hand and prepared to lower his fly zipper with the other. But before Jacob could open the zipper, Juan Diego pulled a switchblade out of his back pocket and jammed it into Jacob's neck.

Juan Diego pulled it out, and blood shot through the air. Jacob put his hand on his neck and tried to scream, but Juan Diego grabbed Jacob's mouth and held it closed. Jacob took a few steps backward, perplexed at what just happened. He could feel the blood ejaculating into his hand and down his neck. It felt warm, almost soothing, but he could not stop the flow.

"What the…" is all Jacob could speak before Juan Diego lunged toward Jacob and forced the bloody blade into Jacob's stomach.

As Juan Diego pulled the knife out of Jacob's stomach, Jacob fell back to the ground, spitting up blood, his body shaking. He tried to stop the blood from escaping the two wounds. He grabbed the clothes on the ground and applied pressure to both holes, but they did little to stop the bleeding. Juan Diego watched as Jacob was covered in blood and dirt.

"Why?" Jacob tried to yell as he spat up more blood.

"Why not?" Juan Diego replied, wiping the blade on the leg of his jeans without thinking about what he was doing. A part of Jacob would leave the scene, after all.

Juan Diego watched Jacob struggle to catch his breath and struggle to move. He watched with a smirk on his face. Juan Diego folded the knife and put it back in his pocket before unzipping his fly and pulling out his penis.

"Is this what you wanted?" he asked Jacob, swinging it around with his hand. "Here you go."

Then Juan Diego peed all over Jacob, smearing his bright yellow with Jacob's dark red, creating a violent swirl of color. Jacob felt the warm wetness on his legs, chest, and face, choking on the warm yellow water.

Juan Diego laughed loudly but was quiet enough not to draw the attention of anyone walking past the brush. He was enjoying watching Jacob drown in pee and blood. After a few minutes, Jacob stopped moving and stopped fighting the inevitable. Juan Diego kicked the limp body before him several times and got no response, so he put his penis back in his pants, picked up the backpack, and walked out of the bushes. As he emerged, he felt the warmth of the midday sun. No one saw Juan Diego as he walked away.

Chapter Twelve

"That is some messed up shit," Oliver said, breaking the silence. "And that is saying something considering all the shit you have put me through these last few years."

"I know," Nicholas replied.

"How could you not tell me this before now?" Oliver asked.

"There was no reason to tell," Nicholas said. "Juan Diego was part of my past, long ago—long before you and I met. I never expected him to resurface after all these years."

"Yes, but if he was that obsessed with you in the past…"

"I thought he was dead!" Nicholas interrupted Oliver. "Years ago, long before you and I met, he found me, tracked me down in London. As I said, he had been following me for years, and after I stopped replying to his gifts of body parts, he showed up at a party I was attending in London. We got into an argument; we became the center of attention at the party, which I did not like at all.

"We argued too much at the party before finally taking the fight outside and down the street toward Hyde Park. He was professing his love for me and demanding I do the same to him. He called me a liar each time I told him that I did not love him, that I loved someone else."

"Who did you love?" Oliver asked.

"We kept arguing," Nicholas continued, ignoring Oliver's question. "And before I knew it, fists were flying. We were beating the shit out of each other. I had no idea how strong he had become.

Ultimately, I swung hard enough to knock him into the Serpentine. I waited and waited, but he never came out of the water. As far as I was concerned, he drowned. After waiting for more than five minutes, I left."

"That is a fucked-up story," Oliver said, hitting Nicholas in the chest. "Your anger issues are not anger issues, are they? You are a straight-up murderer, and I think you like it."

"Listen," Nicholas started to say, rubbing his chest. "I did not set out to kill him, but…"

"You have said that a lot," Oliver interrupted. "You didn't mean to kill anyone, yet you do kill people. Intentional or not, you are still killing people.

"Who did you love so much all those years ago that it drove Juan Diego crazy enough to be still chasing after you now?" Oliver asked. "And please do not lie to me. After all I have put up with because of you; with you — you owe me the truth."

"You," Nicholas said. "I was in love with you. Are you happy? Do you feel better knowing I was in love with you long before you and I met on that park bench? Some might even say that I obsessed with you."

Nicholas sat beside Oliver with his elbows on the table, crying into his hands. He was crying like he had never cried in his life. He had trouble breathing and could not control the tears seeping through his fingers. He could not speak. He tried, but all that came out of his mouth was a mumbled mess of sounds. Nicholas was not used to telling the truth or crying this much. The moment that he had been working up to for years — when he would tell Oliver the truth — was happening now, and he was completely unprepared.

Oliver let Nicholas cry. He wanted to ask more questions but felt he would not get anywhere until Nicholas let it all out. After a few more minutes, Nicholas' loud gasps turned into whimpers, and before he knew it, just a few sniffles.

"Sorry," Nicholas finally said. "I did not mean to break down like that, and I did not want to tell you the truth this way. I am not sure exactly how I imagined it would come out; my loving you for so long, but I am sorry. I am sorry for lying. I am sorry for holding it all back."

Oliver looked at Nicholas, trying to determine if Nicholas was being sincere. He heard the words come out of Nicholas' mouth but wondered if he could tell the truth from the lies. Oliver had become so jaded by Nicholas' lies that he now had trouble comprehending the conversation.

"I know I should have a thousand questions," Oliver responded. "But the truth is I no longer know what to believe or not believe. I have spent what feels like a lifetime on this estate waiting for you. I loved you once; I probably still do, but I need a break now. I cannot keep living a life where any minute it will be turned inside out because of someone or something from your past.

"Murderers? Stalkers? What else are you not telling me about your past?" asked Oliver. "That is rhetorical. It would be best if you did not tell me anything else. I need a normal life. I hoped that a normal life meant you and me, here on this estate or anywhere so long as we were together. But that will not be possible with your dead boyfriend stalking us, will it?

"He was not my…" Nicholas started to say but was interrupted by Oliver.

"I am not done speaking," Oliver yelled, then paused, filling the kitchen air with silence. "Never mind, I am done. I am done with all of it. I am going back to New York in the morning. When you figure out your life, and if you decide that I am the one you love, come home. You know where I will be."

"You can't leave," Nicholas said sternly. "You are the one I love. If you leave before I can end this with Juan Diego, he will follow you, hunt you down to hurt me, and I cannot let that happen."

"This is your problem to solve," Oliver said as he got up. "I will stay at a hotel near the airport tonight."

Before Nicholas could say another word, Oliver was out the kitchen door.

Nicholas slammed his fist on the kitchen table, startling George's mother as she came in to clean up breakfast. George was with her this morning. He wanted to be sure that Nicholas was settling in okay.

"Did I see Mr. Oliver walking down the driveway just now?" George asked.

"Yes, he wants to explore the town," Nicholas lied as he let another tear escape.

Nicholas went outside, leaving George and his mother to clean up. He wanted to chase after Oliver, but he knew that it was fruitless. Oliver wanted space, and Nicholas needed to give that to him. Nicholas knew that until Oliver calmed down, he could not be reasoned with, even if his life was in danger. Instead, Nicholas knew that he needed to find Juan Diego. He knew that until Juan Diego was out of the picture for good, there was no way he and Oliver could ever be together again.

He tried to pinpoint when everything went wrong. In hindsight, Nicholas realized he had taken too long to get to California. He had been overly cautious because he wanted to keep Oliver safe but ended up putting him in more danger. Nicholas could see now that his whole plan backfired since he never expected Juan Diego to resurface.

As usual, Nicholas was not telling the whole truth to Oliver when he said that Juan Diego had drowned. He wished he had drowned. They never argued at a party. They argued for the reasons Nicholas confessed, but it was not as dramatic as his lie to Oliver. All those years ago, Nicholas left Juan Diego lying in a hotel bed, dreaming of the sexual experience they shared that night and so many nights prior.

The following day, Nicholas left the hotel room without leaving a note. Juan Diego was still sleeping soundly. It was the same London trip that Oliver had watched Nicholas murder John Doe in the cemetery. As much as Nicholas enjoyed the surprise of running into Juan Diego then, he was already focused on Oliver and was not interested in welcoming Juan Diego back into his life. He did not know then that Juan Diego had been stalking him almost as long as Nicholas had been stalking Oliver.

As Nicholas sat alone on the porch, he realized he had been a total jerk. He had spent the better part of a decade trying to be with the one man he believed he loved more than any other, and yet he continued to make stupid judgments that made Oliver angry and put Oliver in danger. He knew he needed to go after Oliver, to fight for his love. It was time to tell the truth, the whole truth, and nothing but the truth.

Nicholas jumped out of the rocking chair and ran down the driveway. He was hopeful that Oliver was still walking. At the base of the driveway, Oliver jumped into a cab. He was crying, and he was tired from the long walk.

"To the airport, please," he said as he sat back and closed his eyes.

Nicholas reached the entrance to Redwood Manor as the cab drove away. He yelled, but no one heard him. He knew he needed to catch Oliver, stop him from getting away, and, more importantly, stop him from being killed by Juan Diego.

Chapter Thirteen

By the time Juan Diego reached Cow Hollow, the corner of Golden Gate Park where he had left Jacob was littered with police cars. The dispatcher tried to get Juan Diego to stay on the line so she could get more information from him, but he was only as cooperative as he needed to be.

"There is a naked man covered in blood," Juan Diego cried into the phone, sounding afraid. He used the best midwestern white boy accent he could fake. He even sniffled as if he had been crying. Juan Diego painted a colorful picture that made the dispatcher blush before he hung up the phone, broke it in two, and threw the two pieces in two different directions. He had no intention of letting the police track him, but he want them to have their massacre murderer.

As much as Juan Diego wanted to steal another car, he knew leaving it in Timber Cove would draw police in his direction. Instead, he walked through the city and crossed the Golden Gate Bridge on foot. It took longer than he had wanted, but he knew he needed to take these precautions. On the north end of the Golden Gate Bridge, Juan Diego saw a young couple getting into their car. They had stopped at the visitor parking to enjoy the view across the bay. Juan Diego watched the couple for a moment, then as they were pulling out of the parking lot, he put out his hand, thumb up, hoping that they would give him a ride. The young couple, Betsy and Phil, were from Wisconsin and beginning their month-long honeymoon up the coast.

Sitting in the backseat, Juan Diego listened to the newlyweds sing along to happy love songs. His hosts would pepper Juan Diego with questions and share random facts about themselves between tunes. He watched the two interact with each other. They were happy. They were in love. They were still riding the high from saying 'I do' a day earlier. Juan Diego wanted that feeling, and he wanted it with Nicholas.

Juan Diego did not tell Betsy and Phil he was going to Timber Cover. Instead, he lied about being a tourist heading to Fort Ross, just south of Timber Cover. The newlyweds were thrilled that Fort Ross was on their path, and they filled the two-hour drive with their colorful backstory.

Betsy and Phil started dating in high school, then continued to date through college even though they studied on opposite coasts. In college, they explored their sexuality, settling into the reality that they were both bisexual. Their honesty and comfort with who they were gave each the confidence to be themselves, even if both parents wanted straight, Christian, conservative children.

While studying at Stanford, Phil fell in love with Truman and introduced Truman to Betsy before they all finished their freshman year. Betsy was excited, but it took Truman a little longer to accept the triangle that had formed. Truman was gay; he had been his whole life. He never had sex with a woman, but he was used to sleeping with guys who had been with a girl before or called themselves 'straight' even though they liked dick.

When Phil and Truman first met, Phil made it clear that he was not just exploring his sexuality. He knew what he wanted and knew he would have fun along the way. Phil made it abundantly clear that his future included marrying Betsy, but he had not planned on falling in love with a man—with Truman. The two men, and eventually Betsy, often talked about the love triangle. Truman played along with Phil and Betsy, never thinking anything would continue past freshman year, let alone graduation. Truman assumed he would return to New York and eventually meet his future husband.

The next challenge came in their junior year when Betsy introduced Joanne to the boys. Betsy and Joanne met just before the summer break of their sophomore year, and they stayed in touch through the summer while Betsy and Phil traveled Europe. Halfway through the first semester of junior year, Betsy knew she loved Joanne. She just hoped that Phil would, too.

Like Betsy, Joanne had a long-distance boyfriend all through college. She did not love him like Betsy loved Phil, but he was what she needed while she discovered herself. He was the perfect arm candy for holidays, but ultimately, they would break up before graduation. Joanne was ready to commit herself to a new love.

Phil liked Joanne almost instantly—why wouldn't he, he thought. His girlfriend loved Joanne, so he must, too. Truman took a little longer to come around to liking Joanne as much as Phil and Betsy did. Eventually, the four got along famously. During their senior year spring break, Phil, Truman, Betsy, and Joanne took a vacation together for the first time. Truman was the only one skeptical about the arrangement, but as the four enjoyed a private sailing yacht tour of the Caribbean, it became clear to Phil and Betsy what they wanted. It was on that trip that Phil proposed.

Truman was the best man, and Joanne was the bridesmaid. They were overseeing the wedding clean-up back in Wisconsin and were scheduled to join Phil and Betsy for the latter half of the honeymoon. The marriage had not changed anything regarding how the four felt about each other or about how Phil and Truman or Betsy and Joanne would go on living their lives together.

"And that's us," Betsy sang in her best midwestern twang as she turned around in the front seat to face Juan Diego, getting a good look at him for the first time since he got into the car.

"My, you are a handsome one," she continued. "Isn't he, hun?"

"Yessiree, he is," Phil replied.

"So, the four of you are in a polyamorous relationship?" Juan Diego asked. He had not expected a life story from his temporary hosts and certainly was not expecting one so colorful.

"Yes!" Betsy exclaimed. "And it is so wonderful." She leaned over and kissed Phil on the cheek.

"And what about you?" Phil asked Juan Diego, looking at him through the rearview mirror. "Do you have a special someone waiting for you at Fort Ross?"

Juan Diego held Phil's attention in the mirror. Phil wanted to look away; he knew he needed to so he could focus on the road, but it was as if Juan Diego had him in a trance. Before Juan Diego could answer the question, Betsy screamed louder than she intended, scaring Phil enough to take his eyes off Juan Diego. Phil looked forward, seeing that he had swerved into the oncoming lane. Before he could regain control of the car, it slammed into the guard rail on the opposite side of the road, scraping the railing for several yards before stopping. Phil's door was pinned to the metal barrier—the only thing between the car and a five-hundred-foot drop to the ocean below. The front left tire was hanging over the cliff. Betsy was crying quietly in the passenger's seat while Juan Diego sat silently in the back, glad to be sitting behind Betsy and not Phil.

"Everyone okay?" Phil asked, still shaken by what just happened. He looked at his new bride and then back at Juan Diego. Phil found it creepy that Juan Diego was still looking at him through the rearview mirror, still wearing the same evil expression.

"Let me help you get out safely," Juan Diego said to Phil as he released the seatbelt and stepped out of the car. Ahead, he could see a truck coming towards them quickly. At the same time, Juan Diego looked up and saw some boulders tumbling down the cliff to his right. Instead of helping Phil and Betsy, Juan Diego started running. He wanted to get as far away from the vehicle and the falling boulders as quickly as possible. He managed to get 50 feet from the car when he turned to see two boulders hit the road, each about the same size as six basketballs, bounce off the road and hit the passing truck. The impact flipped the truck towards the guard rails, pushing it into Phil and Betsy's car. On its side, the truck plowed into the passenger door. The impact threw Betsy, who had unlocked her seatbelt moments earlier, towards Phil.

Juan Diego watched the truck push the car through the guard rail and over the cliff. The truck followed. Juan Diego ran back towards where the car once sat, looking at the big hole where the guard rails used to be. Holding on to a secure part of the rail, Juan Diego looked over the edge as best he could. Far below, he could see a twisted pile of metal. He was sure that no one survived the fall.

Juan Diego stepped away from the edge and looked around to see that he was alone. He looked to his left and right, as far out as he could along the winding road dividing the land from the sea. No other cars were coming. He looked at the road and saw the large boulders in the middle. Juan Diego knew the next car might join the others over the cliff if someone did not move the boulders. He did not care.

As he started to walk, Juan Diego realized that his journals and gun were gone. They were in the bag still in the car that was mangled on the rocks far below. He screamed as loud as he could, then started laughing before turning and heading towards Timber Cove. Juan Diego was partially relieved that any evidence linking him to the massacre had been destroyed, and any written evidence of his infatuation with Nicholas and his desire to kill Oliver were washed out to sea.

Chapter Fourteen

When Juan Diego reached Timber Cove, he wondered if Hector's body was still lying in a pool of blood or was now at the center of a CBI investigation. Given the amount of blood on his hands today, Juan Diego did not want to come face to face with the police, so he avoided the motel. He was still quite rattled by the car accident and realized that if he had not gotten out of the car when he did, he would be hanging off the cliff, most likely dead. That would mean never seeing Nicholas again.

Juan Diego sat on a bench in front of the Timber Cove post office. The streets were quiet. In the distance, he could see the entrance to Redwood Manor, its regal stone and iron gates designed to keep people out. They did not do a good job, he thought. As Juan Diego contemplated his next move, he noticed the gates open. A few minutes later, he watched a yellow taxicab drive through the gates and turn south. The cab stopped at the traffic light next to where Juan Diego was sitting.

Nicholas was sitting alone in the cab's backseat when he turned and saw Juan Diego looking back at him. Juan Diego wore a smile as soft and welcoming as he could muster, given how exhausted and frazzled he felt. It took Nicholas a few seconds to recognize that he was looking at a disheveled Juan Diego. Nicholas rolled down the window, and before he could say anything, he heard Juan Diego yell, "I am coming for you, my love."

The light turned green as Juan Diego stood up, and the car sped south. Instead of running after the taxi—after Nicholas, Juan Diego decided to head up to Redwood Manor. He did not see Oliver in the cab and assumed he was still in the house. As tired as Juan Diego was then, he knew he needed to take action. He needed to make a bold move. He believed that kidnapping Oliver was the best way for Nicholas to listen to him.

As he walked the long trek from the gate to the main house, Juan Diego thought about how he would take Oliver alive. He had to take him alive. He knew that Oliver was no good to him dead. He was, but not in the way that would help Juan Diego prove his love to Nicholas. He had not left Oliver on the best of terms the other day, so he knew he needed a new game plan, a better one.

When Juan Diego reached the house, it sat dark, which he thought odd. The sun was about to drop below the horizon as it cast a swatch of vibrant color above the trees. Juan Diego could not see any lights in the house, and there was no activity on the porch. He suddenly thought that maybe he got it wrong. Maybe Oliver was in the car with Nicholas, and Juan Diego did not see him. Juan Diego walked up to the front door and knocked anyway. He needed to be sure.

After a few more knocks, Juan Diego was getting irritated. He was angry with himself for not taking Oliver captive the other day. He was angry at himself for letting this entire chase go on for as long as it had. He started to walk back down the front steps when the door opened. He turned around to find an old woman standing, holding a dish rag.

Juan Diego asked a question, but the woman only looked back at him. Then he spoke in Spanish, and the two were firing questions and answers back and forth. George's mother did not know where Oliver or Nicholas was. She yelled through the house, calling for George in hopes that he would have more information. He did not, or at least if he did; he was not about to share that information with a stranger.

"I am sorry, my friend," George said to Juan Diego as he joined his mother at the front door. "They are not home, and I am unsure when they will return. If you leave me your name and number, I will let them know you stopped by."

Juan Diego stood at the door listening to George, studying him, trying to determine how strong he might be. Juan Diego knew that it was time to make a statement to Nicholas, a loud one, and maybe that statement did not need to be kidnapping Oliver. Instead, Juan Diego decided that spilling more blood would send Nicholas a more unmistakable message.

By now, George's mother had retreated into the depths of the house. Standing before George, Juan Diego decided that George might not be that big of a challenge, so he pushed the door open and lunged towards George. He swung and was surprised at how slowly George moved, accepting the right fist that forced his nose to fire blood toward the door. George fell back into the foyer and to the floor. Juan Diego pulled a knife from his pocket before diving toward George, slicing his neck open. Still adjusting to the pain of his broken nose, George grabbed his neck, struggling to keep the blood from gushing out. Before George stopped breathing, Juan Diego was already moving through the house.

George's mother was already running back toward the front of the house to investigate all the loud thuds she heard. As she ran towards the front, Juan Diego was running towards her, and his knife went into her stomach a few times before he punched her face, knocking her to the floor. Mother and son were trounced, lying not far from each other, making a big mess on the floor that George's mother spent so much time cleaning each day.

Juan Diego kicked the old woman's body as it lay lifeless on the floor and then he walked into the kitchen to wash the blood off his hands. Sitting down to figure out his next move, he saw the satellite phone on the counter. He picked it up and saw a number on the screen displaying the last incoming call. Juan Diego took a chance and dialed that number back.

"Hi, babe," Nicholas spat into the phone once he answered. He was excited to see the satellite phone number, hoping Oliver had returned home.

"You never called me babe," Juan Diego said back. "That is a little too sappy even for you, Nick."

"I thought that was you on the bench, JD," Nicholas said. "What are you doing in my house?"

"I was hoping to chat with Oliver after seeing you leave," Juan Diego said. "But he is not here. Where is he, Nick?"

"You should not have shown up at my house," Nicholas said. "I told you more than once that we are done—we never really were a couple. You need to move on and leave Oliver alone. You need to leave me alone, too."

"Sorry, Nick, but you know I am not going to do that," Juan Diego replied, getting upset with Nicholas. "I promised you I would kill everyone you loved so we could be together, and I intend to keep that promise.

"Oh yeah, and you might want a new cleaning crew. The two you have here are staining the floors red right now."

"What did you do, JD?" Nicholas asked, yelling into the phone, startling his driver.

"Keeping my promise, my love," Juan Diego sang back. "Where are you?"

"You know I am in a car," Nicholas said. "You saw me drive by."

"Don't be an asshole, Nick," Juan Diego said. "When will you be back?"

"Not anytime soon," Nicholas said as he hung up the phone. He wished he knew how to get a hold of Oliver, to warn Oliver not to return to Redwood Manor, not that he would. Nicholas was sure Oliver was sticking to his word and was safely in a hotel, waiting for the next flight back to New York.

Furious at Nicholas for hanging up on him, Juan Diego threw the phone across the kitchen, pulled the stove away from the wall, and snapped the gas line. He franticly rummaged through the house, looking for anything with Nicholas's scent. He wanted to smell Nicholas. He missed that lovely aroma that lingered on Nicholas' skin. Juan Diego eventually found a T-shirt on a bedroom floor. He picked it up and shoved it into his face, taking in the sweaty hints of eucalyptus and sandalwood. When he pulled the shirt away from his nose, Juan Diego could smell gas swimming through the rooms. He covered his face with the T-shirt and ran downstairs to the front door. As he walked out of the house, Juan Diego lit a match and threw it back into the house. He barely made it across the porch before he heard the explosion; he felt it as it pushed him through the air.

Fifteen minutes later, Juan Diego woke up. His head and back hurt. He had been thrown twenty feet before landing on the grass, well beyond the edge of the porch. His ears were still ringing. He looked behind him to see the main house burning brightly. The explosion had sent some parts of the house towards the forest surrounding the house, catching the trees on fire, too. He stood up, examining himself to be sure his pain was from the impact and not something more serious.

He watched the fire for a few minutes and then started down the drive back toward the front gate. He did not want to be on site when the fire department arrived. Halfway down the driveway, Juan Diego heard sirens in the distance. Given its isolation, he wondered how anyone could have known about the house fire so quickly. But then he stopped and looked around to see that the whole forest was on fire and catching up to him quickly. The sky became a giant black cloud that he was sure could be seen for miles. He ran.

Juan Diego took a chance and returned to his motel room before fire and police arrived at Redwood Manor. He was surprised that the 'Do Not Disturb" sign was still hanging on the door handle. The stench of Hector's dead body attacked him as soon as he opened the door. He quickly closed the door and headed to the bathroom to shower. The television was still on from earlier that morning. He had no intention of staying in the room any longer than necessary.

When Juan Diego came out of the shower, he saw the news. Redwood Manor was on fire. Within the first 90 minutes, more than 1000 acres were ablaze. Juan Diego knew that Nicholas would not be happy, and he hoped that Nicholas would think that Juan Diego had killed Oliver. Only Nicholas knew that Oliver was safe.

Juan Diego got dressed and left the motel room again, purposely forgetting to put the 'Do Not Disturb' sign on the door. He was not returning for sure this time, and it was time someone found Hector. Juan Diego approached the town square to look for another car to steal.

Chapter Fifteen

When the police arrived at Golden Gate Park, they found Jacob's body in the bushes, just as their anonymous caller said they would. Seeing Jacob's naked body on the ground, covered in dirt and blood, the officers immediately assumed drugs or prostitution were to blame. It was not often that someone called the police to report a dead body in the park. The police were used to being called to break up fights or even bust a drug deal, so they were a little unprepared to find Jacob's body as beaten and bloody as it was, even though Juan Diego made it abundantly clear when he spoke with the 9-1-1 operator.

Two officers assigned to the case were rookies and had never seen a dead body before, at least not up close and in person. The first to walk through the bushes vomited almost immediately, ruining part of the crime scene. Her lunch burrito with extra salsa only added to the red mess before her. The second officer ran out of the bushes to throw up her lunch. The third officer was the most senior. He had been on the job for an entire year and had seen his share of dead bodies in the Tenderloin, but those were mostly drug overdoses. Even he was taken aback by all the blood in front of him.

Once the three recomposed themselves and prepared to look closely at Jacob's body, they found a wallet in the backpack that Juan Diego left behind. The wallet was empty except for a driver's license and a health insurance card. Both had the same name: Jacob Jackson Smithers, III of Greenwich, Connecticut. The baby-faced photo seemed happy, excited even, which was a far cry from the wounded, hardened face on the ground. One officer called the station and gave them Jacob's name and driver's license number, hoping they were not fake. He had no criminal record, but Jacob was listed as a runaway in the national database of missing children. That is where they found a Connecticut phone number. Officer Stevenson dreaded the call he was going to have to make, but he knew this was the ugly side of his job.

* * * * *

Jacob and his father were not close. They lived together and loved one another, but Jacob's mother died of a heart attack when he was 13, which put a greater strain on the relationship between him, his father, and his older brother. Fighting often led to yelling and sometimes hitting. Mr. Smithers never meant to hit his sons, not intentionally. He was not a bad person, not a bad dad. He was just not equipped to be the primary parent; that had always been his wife's role, and she played it almost too well. She was the perfect wife and mother who over-coddled her children, especially Jacob.

When she died, all three of her boys lost their way. Mr. Smithers took the longest to recover, which made the teen years for Jacob and his brother Ethan difficult. Ethan was a junior in high school when his mother died, so by the time he was done mourning, he was off to college. Jacob, however, still had another four years alone with his parentally challenged father.

Between his dad's lack of parenting and the influx of his new girlfriends, each trying to fill the new mom role, Jacob could not handle living with his father anymore. One day, he woke up and got dressed for school as he had done so many days before, but this time he packed a few extra items. He said goodbye to his father and walked out the front door, skipping breakfast like he did most other days.

Jacob was not present when the morning bell rang and roll call began. Following protocol, the school called Mr. Smithers looking for Jacob. He was surprised to get the call since he remembered watching his son head off to school that morning. Mr. Smithers called Jacob's phone, but it went straight to voicemail. Panicked and afraid that something might have happen to Jacob; that maybe he was hurt, Mr. Smithers left work and returned home to an empty house. He called Jacob's phone again and found it in Jacob's bedroom, under his pillow. Mr. Smithers called his son Ethan, who had not heard from Jacob either. Neither Smithers man knew where Jacob had wandered off to nor had they paid enough attention to know that Jacob was suffering, suffocating without his mother. There was no note. Jacob was just gone.

Mr. Smithers and the police spent months looking for Jacob. Ethan came home from college to help and while Mr. Smithers and Ethan refused to stop looking for Jacob, the police did. After two months with no leads, the Greenwich police entered Jacob's name into the national database of missing children with hopes that someone would see Jacob or know something. No one ever did until now. If it weren't for Juan Diego, Mr. Smithers might never have seen his baby boy again.

* * * * *

Mr. Smithers received several calls over the year from different police departments with what they thought could be positive leads on Jacob, but nothing ever came to fruition. This time was different. This was the phone call he hoped he would never receive.

"Mr. Smithers?" asked Officer Stevenson.

"Yes," he replied, waiting for what he hoped would be good news.

"This is Officer Stevenson of the San Francisco police department. I am afraid that I have some bad news, sir."

Before the officer could say anything more, he could hear Mr. Smithers crying loudly through the receiver. Mr. Smithers handed the phone to Ethan, who was back home again; he just graduated from Rhode Island College. Ethan continued to talk with Officer Stevenson, answering a series of questions to help the officer determine that the dead body in his custody was Ethan's brother. Office Stevenson told Ethan that once his department could finish processing Jacob's body, they would schedule a video viewing so Ethan and his father could identify and confirm that the dead body was, in fact, Jacob.

It would take another few days before the police could pin the massacre on Jacob. That was going to be another call that Mr. Smithers would not be prepared to take.

* * * * *

While there was a plethora of camera footage capturing the intersection where Jacob sat day after day, it would take some time for the police to identify and apprehend their killer. They had a clear image of the boy responsible for the destruction, but the image alone would not help solve their case. By the second day, the officers working the massacre began distributing grainy images of Jacob to the media. The CBI and FBI joined the task force created to bring their suspect to justice.

When the officers found Jacob's naked, bruised body in Golden Gate Park, the grainy photo of Jacob had not yet been circulated. The next day, when Jacob's body was being prepped so it could be viewed by Mr. Smithers, the technician cleaning Jacob's face was spooked. She had seen that same face on the news for the last 24 hours. She called her supervisor, who called the police back to the morgue. It was possible that they had captured their killer after all.

A separate group of police officers, along with FBI Agent Calvin Dunraven, were trying to determine how their unnamed suspect had obtained an illegal weapon, by California rules anyway, what happened to the gun, and more importantly, where the killer was hiding out. It was clear from the camera footage that Jacob acted alone, at least in pulling the trigger, but the authorities were convinced that someone else had to be involved. They watched hours of footage and day after day the grainy, skinny white boy never looked like a threat; never looked like someone capable of owning or even gaining access to such a powerful weapon. Agent Dunraven became convinced that someone supplied the gun and probably still had the gun.

By the time that Agent Dunraven painted a picture of who the killer was the local police shared that they had their killer in custody, in the morgue. Agent Dunraven was excited to give the grainy boy image a name; glad to be able to assign blame for the massacre. He was not excited that Jacob was dead though. To Agent Dunraven, this was yet another twist in yet another case among a growing list of cases where dead bodies were surfacing up and down the west coast. Agent Dunraven was convinced that many of the cases were connected, and he now believed that Jacob's case was connected, too.

Dozens of fingerprints were taken from Jacob's body, his backpack, and the clothes found at the crime scene. The high school kid, Marc, who owned the clothes and backpack, was not helpful. His prints were all over the bag and clothes, of course, and he was in the system because all California children under 13 were fingerprinted through a state-wide program aimed at protecting young children.

When Marc's mug came up on the screen, the officer helping with the case was shocked. She was neighbors with this boy. She saw him often, so she offered to speak with him and his parents, and in doing so, she learned about the bullying and lost backpack. The officer was surprised to learn that Marc's parents had not come forward about their son being bullied. They were notorious for calling the police anytime someone looked at their darling child wrong. But the truth was that Marc had not told his parents that he was being bullied or why he was being bullied. Marc knew that if he told his conservative Catholic parents that he was gay, the bullying by kids at school would be nothing compared to how his parents would treat him.

While interviewing Marc and his parents, the police shared a photo of Jacob in hopes that they might recognize him, but they did not. With Marc no longer a person of interest, the police continued down their list: everyone whose fingerprints were found on Jacob. The next set of fingerprints pulled off Jacob's body were a match to

Juan Diego. He made the fatal error of touching Jacob, kissing him, and then holding his torso as he plunged the switchblade into Jacob's stomach. Juan Diego never thought that his fingerprints would be found, could be found, but they were sealed in blood, creating a perfect mold for the FBI.

Unfortunately for Juan Diego, he was not as slick as Nicholas when it came to avoiding the police. When Juan Diego was 15, he was once again accused of killing a boy. This was not new for Juan Diego and his family, but this time, he was old enough for the Judge to consider him an adult. Juan Diego was convicted, fingerprinted, and put into the system. He spent three weeks in jail and was later acquitted, but his records were never expunged. That was almost a decade ago. When the police ran the prints found on Jacob's body, Juan Diego's baby-faced teenage mugshot filled the screen. He looked younger than Marc. The last known address for Juan Diego was his parents' house in Arizona.

Armed with this new information, Agent Dunraven called the Phoenix police department. It had been ten years since the photo was taken and Agent Dunraven was certain that Juan Diego did not look the same as the image on the computer screen. He was not expecting the officers to find Juan Diego in Phoenix, especially since his fresh fingerprints were all over Jacob in San Francisco, but he was leaving no stone unturned.

Agent Dunraven sent the photo of Juan Diego to Phoenix and the station sent two officers to the last known address for Juan Diego. The officers were not prepared to have an older version of the photo greet them at the door.

"Hello officers," Javier said as he pulled the front door of his mother's apartment wide open. "How can I help you?"

"Put your hands where we can see them," the first officer yelled.

Javier complied. He was used to altercations with the police. They often confused Javier with Juan Diego or Pedro. Before the police could take any drastic actions against Javier, his mother came to the door.

"Officers, please put your guns away and release my Javier," his mother pleaded. "Once again you have mistaken him for one of his brothers, no doubt."

The officers did not release Javier. Instead, the put him in hand cuffs and sat him on the ground while they spoke with Javier's mother. In those discussions they learned that Javier was not Juan Diego and that Juan Diego had left home after high school. He moved out and never wrote, called, or made any contact. She did tell the police that an envelope full of cash would periodically arrive in the mail. She knew it was from Juan Diego, but every envelope was blank except for her address, so she never knew where Juan Diego was or how he came into all the cash he sent. But she knew in her heart that it was from her baby.

The officers took the most recent envelope that Juan Diego's mother received. She pulled the money out of the envelope before giving the empty envelope to the officers. She had no idea that the money belonged to Xiang, but that did not matter yet. The police had not connected that many dots just yet, but they were hopeful that they could pull prints or DNA off the envelope to better connect Juan Diego to Jacob's murder.

With all this new information, Agent Dunraven had to assume that Juan Diego was still in San Francisco. With Juan Diego being the only lead they had in the death of Jacob, and possibly the only lead they had to charge someone with the massacre, Agent Dunraven reluctantly made a statement to the press, putting Juan Diego's face and name everywhere in hopes that someone would come forward with any information to help them solve both crimes.

Some 2,500 miles away, busy trying to solve his own set of cases around a series of murders, FBI Agent Edward Dalrymple watched Agent Dunraven on television. Agent Dalrymple looked closely at the necktie Agent Dunraven was wearing in the press conference. It still had a large dark spot near the base from where Agent Dalrymple had spilled red wine on it when the two were enjoying a weekend away together. These days, it was more challenging for Calvin and Edward to put down their badges and be themselves together. Eddie smiled and shook his head. He thought he had thrown that necktie away before he kissed Calvin goodbye a month ago.

Chapter Sixteen

It had been three days since Juan Diego torched Redwood Manor and fled south. After spending a day roaming San Francisco, trying to collect his thoughts and recall his master plan, he found himself holed up in a hotel in Burlingame, trying to formulate his next move. He was furious at everyone for derailing his plans.

The following day, Juan Diego woke up to see his face on the television screen, or at least a baby-faced version of a younger Juan Diego. Juan Diego looked into the mirror hanging above the television to compare what he saw with what was on the screen. There was a minimal resemblance now. Juan Diego still looked like a teenager – maybe a more mature one, but the image on the screen looked more like Juan Diego's father when he was younger and alive.

Starring at the young man looking back at him, Juan Diego angrily punched the mirror. As the cracked lines moved out in multiple directions, he looked at the blood seeping from his knuckles and contemplated how his plan had come unwoven. He believed it all began with Xiang's death, but he was starting to think it might have been falling apart long before then. He had always intended to kill Xiang, but how and when it happened was not part of his master plan. If Xiang had just stayed in the basement, Juan Diego's gun would never have ended up in the hands of Jacob, and the massacre might never have happened; it would not have happened. With no massacre, Juan Diego and Jacob would not have met, and Juan Diego was confident that had it played out correctly, his face would not be all over the news now. And after all that, Juan Diego still refused to admit he was to blame.

Sitting on the edge of the bed, exhausted and dripping blood on the sheets, Juan Diego did not care that he was making a mess of the hotel room, but he should have cared. He was leaving more DNA, extending the breadcrumb trail for the FBI to find him. He was no closer to being with Nicholas, yet the shadow of death behind him was full of bodies. As Juan Diego licked his knuckles, enjoying the taste of his blood, he was reminded of the day at summer camp when he and Nicholas were chasing each other in the woods.

Juan Diego had tripped on a tree root and fell to the ground. Nicholas picked him up and noticed the blood on Juan Diego's hand. Nicholas licked the blood off Juan Diego's palm and kissed the wound as if he could magically heal it. He did not, but that was when Juan Diego realized that Nicholas was the man he wanted to spend the rest of his life with.

As he tasted his blood, thinking of Nicholas, Juan Diego knew it was time to refocus, stop being distracted by all the noise around him, and get back to his goal of being with Nicholas. It had been days since he last saw Nicholas or Oliver, and with Redwood Manor destroyed, he felt confident that Nicholas and Oliver had retreated to New York. His current problem remained the image being blasted across the television screen.

Juan Diego knew that if his name and the photo were on the local news, he would not be able to get on a plane. He wondered if buses and trains would be equally challenging, if he were on national news, or if the issue was contained locally. Ultimately, he decided that he would have to drive, at least out of California, if he were going to get back to New York. Even without knowing if Nicholas and

Oliver were there now, Juan Diego felt confident that one of them would end up back in New York City or maybe even Greenwich again soon. He had been patient for so many years, sitting in the shadows, and he was prepared to be that patient again if it meant staying the course.

After showering and bandaging his hand, Juan Diego headed to the lobby. He put the "Do Not Disturb" sign on the outside of the door, hoping that would delay anyone accessing his room and seeing the destruction, the blood. Then he walked out the front door of the hotel. As he did, a Silicon Valley VC stepped out of his Lamborghini and threw the keys at Juan Diego.

"Park it up front, Amigo," the man said. "I will not be here too long."

Juan Diego thought it was too flashy of a car to escape California, but he knew he could get farther away from the city and improvise along the way.

"Si Senor," Juan Diego threw back at the man as he accepted the keys and a $20 tip.

Juan Diego stepped into the classic yellow sports car and drove off. Three hours later, when the man came out to retrieve his car with a big-breasted blonde hooker under his arm, Juan Diego was more than halfway to Nevada, careful not to speed or draw attention to himself.

The police found the car two days later in Truckee when the local police ran the license number because the car was illegally parked. Juan Diego, however, was east of Denver, riding shotgun with a 65-year-old trucker named Sallie. She was his entertainment until they reached the outskirts of Chicago.

Fortunately for Juan Diego, Sallie did not watch or listen to the news in her rig; it was all fake news to her anyway. Sallie thought she was keeping company with a young college boy heading home to see his family in the Windy City.

Sallie and Juan Diego met in a highway diner off I-80, where Juan Diego sat in a booth, trying to figure out the next leg of his journey east. Sallie saw Juan Diego alone and deep in thought, and before he could say anything, she sat in his booth and started talking to him like a mother talking to a son in distress. He lied about his plans and situation, and Sallie soaked every word. She was desperate for company on the open road.

Sallie spoke like she had smoked a carton of cigarettes every week her entire life. The deep, raspy sound that vibrated from her lips surprised Juan Diego each time she said anything, which was often. As they drove along the highway, Juan Diego wanted to sleep, but Sallie wanted to narrate her life story, starting with her first boyfriend and finishing with her current wife, her third one. Sallie had picked up many hitchhikers over the years, but none traveled the distance that Juan Diego did, so she was excited to have an audience on her long, lonely journey.

Juan Diego shared as little about him as he could, mostly because he was not in the mood to make up an elaborate backstory for Sallie. And that was fine since she did most of the talking. And before he knew it, they were outside of Chicago.

Juan Diego sat patiently as Sallie unhooked her trailer just west of Chicago; not her trailer, but the Pepsi-owned one she had been towing since San Diego. She was so close to being done. The last leg of her trip was just another five hours to Cleveland to be home again with her wife, Julianna. Sallie talked so much about Julianna that Juan Diego felt he already knew her.

As Sallie signed off on the last of the paperwork, she looked back into the cab to see Juan Diego still sitting patiently. By now, Sallie had learned that Chicago was not where Juan Diego was headed; he was set on making it to New York City. She enjoyed the company and was thrilled to have Juan Diego's company for another five hours.

With the cab refueled, the two were back on the road. An hour later, they stopped at a rest area; the three cans of Pepsi Sallie chugged were pushing on her bladder. While Sallie was in the bathroom, Juan Diego spotted a young couple on a bench at the far side of the parking lot. They watched the sunset over the water retention pond at the rest area. Their car was parked near the bathrooms, and Juan Diego noticed no other vehicles.

By now, Juan Diego was well rested. His plan had been reformulated, and he knew how to get Nicholas back. Clearheaded, he stepped out of the cab, grabbing a crowbar from the ass of the truck as he walked toward the couple. By the time the couple realized Juan Diego was behind them, he had smashed both heads. Blood was all over the picnic table and all over Juan Diego. The girl's body fell off the table and was contorted on the ground, her legs tangled on the bench. The boy's body lay across the picnic table, almost suspended since his feet had been tucked under the bench before him. They both screamed when the cold metal split their heads open, but only Juan Diego was around to hear their cries. The girl was knocked unconscious as she hit the ground, but the boy begged Juan Diego to stop, to let them live. He did not listen.

Juan Diego pulled the keys and a wallet out of the dead boy's pants, lifted the crowbar over his head, and slammed it down on the dying boy's chest, snapping his spine. The girl died instantly, never letting another sound escape her small frame. The boy let one final scream out as the crowbar carved a hole in his chest. Blood continued to spew in every direction, continuing to bathe Juan Diego.

When Juan Diego turned back toward the truck, he saw Sallie looking directly at him, in shock at what she witnessed. He ran towards her as she fumbled to get back into the rig. But before Sallie could open the door, Juan Diego jammed the crowbar in Sallie's back. He used so much force that the bar punctured Sallie's shoulder blade before piercing her heart and getting stuck in the closed cab door. Juan Diego left Sallie suspended from the cab door to bleed out.

"Thanks for the ride," Juan Diego whispered into her ear as he further twisted the crowbar. I'll tell Julianna you will be late for dinner."

Sallie screamed and begged Juan Diego to leave Julianna alone before her body finally stopped spitting out words, her final breath begging Juan Diego to stop. Juan Diego had no intention of hurting Julianna. He had no idea where she lived or where Sallie was headed. He said those words because he knew it would add pain to Sallie's final moments.

Juan Diego grabbed any money in Sallie's pockets and combined it with the wallet he pulled from the boy. With $650 in cash, he headed to the bathroom to clean up before driving away in the boy's convertible. With the wind in his hair, Juan Diego set his sights on the Big Apple and finding the love of his life.

Chapter Seventeen

It took Nicholas much longer than Oliver to return to New York. He watched Oliver board a plane and then watched the plane go down the runway and get lost in the clouds. Nicholas should have jumped on the next flight to NYC—there was one boarding two gates down from where he watched Oliver leave, but he did not. Nicholas was afraid to fly directly into any of the New York area airports for fear of being arrested. The last time he was in New England, he blew up Oliver's house, killing several police officers in the process. He knew he was still a wanted man there, so he skipped across the country, making multiple stops in smaller airports before finally renting a car for the last leg of the trip.

Soon after settling into a hotel near Oliver's apartment, Nicholas returned to watching Oliver from afar. He thought about calling Oliver or even knocking on his door to hug him and tell him how sorry he was, but he was worried that Oliver might still be mad. If only he knew how much Oliver longed for him.

As Oliver sat at his kitchen table sipping his morning tea, he saw an open bottle of Old Vine Zin standing alone on the counter. He could see that the bottle was almost empty, and he remembered when he and Nicholas had started to enjoy its contents. He knew it would smell horrid if he pulled the cracked cork out. It had been almost a year since they opened that bottle to celebrate their future life together at Redwood Manor.

He silently cried into his tea and wondered why he still felt so passionately about Nicholas. Oliver knew that Nicholas had made his life a living hell. He knew their relationship was toxic, but there was something about how Nicholas smelt and felt: Nicholas comforted Oliver in a way that Oliver struggled to put into words, and he longed to be with Nicholas when they were apart, even now.

For a moment, Oliver wished Nicholas was sitting with him at the table, maybe even holding hands. He wanted that comfort again; he almost needed it, like a drug. As he relived the last few days at Redwood Manor, Oliver was reminded about Juan Diego and wished that Nicholas had been more honest about Juan Diego. He wondered if he could ever forgive Nicholas or if it mattered anymore. Had he blown it all out of proportion, he asked himself. Everyone has skeletons in their closet; he knew that. He had many himself. At that moment, sitting alone with his tea, Oliver decided to either find Nicholas and be with him forever or forget about everything and move on with his life. He started to build a pros and cons list in his head.

Thirteen floors below, Nicholas sat at a small table in the coffee shop where he sat so many times before. He sipped his black tea, a shift from coffee thanks to Oliver. Even apart, Oliver influenced him. Nicholas knew Oliver was home. He was watching him on the small screen he held in his hands. The two cameras Nicholas installed in Oliver's apartment more than a year ago were still active, giving Nicholas a clear, silent view into Oliver's life, at least in the apartment. As he watched Oliver cry, Nicholas wished he could be in the apartment with Oliver, holding Oliver's hand, letting him know everything would be okay.

As Nicholas finished his tea, he decided today was the day he would speak with Oliver. His confidence was high, and he thought Oliver looked sad and lonely through the grainy live feed on his phone screen. As Nicholas stood up to leave, he looked out the front window of the coffee shop and saw Juan Diego.

"What the F—," Nicholas started, stopping himself from dropping the f-bomb in front of a group of teenage girls walking in for a pre-school latte.

He watched as a figure that looked suspiciously like Juan Diego walked towards Oliver's building. He was still angry with Juan Diego for showing up in California and scaring Oliver. Nicholas blamed Juan Diego for Oliver's sudden departure from Redwood Manor. As he watched the man walk closer to Oliver's building, Nicholas convinced himself that if it was Juan Diego and he was in New York to kill Oliver so he could be with Nicholas again. He had to stop Juan Diego.

Dressed like a flower delivery person, Juan Diego held an oversized floral arrangement in an ornate vase in his hands—something that drew a lot of attention to himself, which Nicholas found odd. It was as if Juan Diego was taunting Nicholas; as if he knew Nicholas was in the coffee shop watching Oliver, watching for Juan Diego. Neither Nicholas nor Oliver knew that Juan Diego had been in town for weeks, watching them both.

Nicholas noticed that a new doorman was on duty at Oliver's building, which meant getting in to see Oliver would be easier for him. He had convinced himself that the last doorman did not like him—he used to give Nicholas a hard time every time he showed up to see Oliver. As soon as Juan Diego disappeared through the building doors, Nicholas decided to call Oliver's old cell phone. He was hopeful that he still had it with him."

"I am not ..." Oliver started to say into the phone before Nicholas cut him off."

"Juan Diego is in your building," Nicholas yelled. "Do not answer the door. I just saw your doorman let him in with a bunch of flowers."

"I am hanging up and calling the police," Oliver fired back.

"Don't call the police," Nicholas replied." I am in the coffee shop downstairs. I was preparing to come up to see you. We need to talk."

"What do you mean, don't call the police?" Oliver yelled. "You have got to be kidding me. I am so tired of all your shit."

Oliver hung up on Nicholas. He was about to call the police and then thought about what he would say and how he would convince them that someone might be pretending to deliver flowers so they could kill him. The more Oliver said it out loud, the more absurd it all sounded. He screamed, then picked his phone up and tapped the number that had just called him."

"What do I do?" Oliver asked before Nicholas could say anything.

"Stay in your apartment," Nicholas said. "Lock the door, then go to the bedroom. I am coming up. Do not let anyone in. I will call you when I am at your front door."

Nicholas hung up and ran out of the coffee shop. He told the new doorman that he was visiting Oliver and was expected. The doorman did not care. He still called up to Oliver.

"Yes sir, thank you. I will send him up," the doorman said into his phone. "You can go up now."

"Thank you," Nicholas said to the doorman. "Oh, one question about the huge floral arrangement that just came in... can you tell me who that was going to?"

"Turn around," the doorman said. That is when Nicholas noticed the large arrangement on the table in the center of the lobby.

"Where did the delivery man go?" Nicholas asked.

"He is in the toilet around the corner," the doorman replied, pointing towards the restrooms, suddenly realizing that the delivery man had been in there longer than expected.

"Call the police," Nicholas said to the doorman. "That is not a delivery man. He is here to murder one of your residents."

"What do you mean murder?" he asked, almost confused by the concept. "Murder who?"

"The person you just called," Nicholas yelled back. "Check the toilet after calling the police. I am going up to see Mr. McPherson."

Nicholas took the elevator to the twelfth floor, then took the stairs up to the thirteenth. While in the stairwell, he looked up and down to see if he could see anyone or hear any movement. The stairwell was silent. When Nicholas opened the door to the thirteenth floor, he saw Juan Diego standing in front of Oliver's door.

"It took you long enough, Nick," Juan Diego said.

"What are you doing, JD," Nicholas asked, slightly out of breath.

"I told you that I was going to kill anyone who got in the way of us being together," Juan Diego said, almost singing his words. "And I meant it. You might be surprised by the number of people who have died for our love — my love, so far."

"You have to stop," Nicholas said. "What you and I had, what we did as teenagers—that was long ago. We were kids."

"We were not kids in London a few years ago," Juan Diego said, getting frustrated with Nicholas. "I recall some amazingly passionate sex—a real connection between us. A reconnection, if you think about it."

"That was rage," Nicholas said.

"Yeah, well, whatever it was," Juan Diego started. "We fucked the shit out of each other, and we both liked it. You even said you loved me, so stop lying to yourself and admit that we are good for each other."

"I am not going to play these games anymore, JD," Nicholas said. "The doorman has called the police, so you must leave before getting arrested."

"Me, arrested," Juan Diego asked, interrupting Nicholas. "Do you want me to tell the police, or better yet, your boy toy on the other side of this door, that you are the one who killed Elizabeth?"

"You do not know what you are talking about," Nicholas yelled.

"You can play dumb or innocent or whatever you think you are playing," Juan Diego continued. "I was there. I helped you kill her, and I will tell everyone, starting with Oliver."

Juan Diego turned to knock on Oliver's door but stopped when he heard Nicholas speak again.

"He is not home," Nicholas lied, trying to distract Juan Diego.

"You think you are the only one who watches him, Nick?" Juan Diego asked, laughing. "This boy has made you soft."

Nicholas stood looking at Juan Diego, trying to find the right words. He needed Juan Diego to leave; he needed to protect Oliver at all costs, so he did what he did best. He lied some more.

"This is between you and me," Nicholas said. "Why don't you and I get out of here and work this out? We do not need to involve Oliver or the police, or anyone for that matter."

"Tell me you love me right now, and I will leave, but only with you," Juan Diego said. "I am a man of my word, Nick. You know that. So, this is all on you."

Nicholas contemplated his following words carefully.

"I love you. There. Let's go." Nicholas said as he reached out his hand.

Juan Diego studied Nicholas' face and body language to determine if he was telling the truth. He knew that Nicholas was lying, most likely, but he liked hearing those three little words. He knew that he had forced Nicholas to say them, but he was confident that he could get Nicholas to repeat them if he could only show Nicholas how much he was loved. Juan Diego slowly stepped away from Oliver's door and toward Nicholas, grabbing Nicholas' hand.

"How will we get out of here if the police are coming?" Juan Diego asked sarcastically.

Nicholas did not answer. Instead, he held Juan Diego's hand tightly, pulling him into the stairwell. They walked down three flights of stairs before exiting onto the tenth floor. They continued down the hall.

"Are we going to escape like petty criminals through some fire escape?" Juan Diego asked, trying to lighten the mood.

Before Nicholas could answer Juan Diego, Nicholas stopped

in front of an apartment door. He pulled a key out of his pocket and unlocked the door. He swung it open and entered, pulling Juan Diego in with him.

"You sly dog," Juan Diego said. "You live three floors below him. That is smart."

"No," Nicholas said. "The owner is out of town, and I have a master key. Now shut up."

Nicholas kissed Juan Diego, knowing that would quiet him and get him to listen. Juan Diego reciprocated with more force and passion than Nicholas had expected; than he had wanted, but Nicholas knew that he opened Pandora's Box to distract Juan Diego. Now, he was paying that price.

"Where is the bedroom?" Juan Diego asked as he started undressing Nicholas in the foyer.

Chapter Eighteen

The apartment Nicholas and Juan Diego were hiding in belonged to William Walker, a successful art dealer in his late 60s whom Nicholas met years ago at an art opening. Back then, Nicholas frequently traveled to Manhattan to explore his sexuality and to find easy targets in the big city; some for sex and others to kill. Nicholas had been walking past an art gallery lit up with a flurry of activity; the next big name in art was showcasing abstract paintings of nude men. The party took over the sidewalk, which is where Nicholas bumped into William, spilling a warm Rose down William's purple suede dinner jacket. William turned around to find Nicholas, young, handsome and almost innocent looking, staring back at him. Before William could get his barrage of foul words out of his mouth, he was choking them back and smiling. William was a sucker for young boy and Nicholas took advantage of that weakness, a lot.

Nicholas spent many nights in the bed he and Juan Diego now lay in. Sometimes, it would be he and the old man, and sometimes, a third or fourth would join in on the fun. William liked to be surrounded by pretty boys—models, prostitutes, it did not matter so long as they were willing to satisfy William's twink thirst. For the right price, they all did. Like Juan Diego, William needed constant affirmation.

As Nicholas lay in the bed now, naked and sticky, he recalled when he was last in this position, in this bed. It was the last time he ruffled the sheets with William and William's favorite Asian rent boy,

Luke. After an evening of debauchery, Nicholas and Luke left William exhausted and half asleep in bed, drained. The two boys got what they wanted that night—gave William what he wanted, but they were hungry for more. Luke and Nicholas walked out of William's apartment together with plans of hitting up a few night clubs—they never did. Nicholas eventually made it back to Greenwich the next morning. Luke never made it home. His body was discovered a week later, mutilated in a dumpster.

    The apartment walls were decorated with paintings of nude men and women, each wrapped in an ornate golden frame. The foyer and living room were filled with marble statues of naked Roman Gods whose names Nicholas could not remember. Apollo, Eros, Himeros, Pothos, and others guarded the apartment, but to Nicholas, they were just nude statues, marble versions of overly defined men with unrealistic physiques. Nicholas remembers the lectures William would give he, Luke, and any other rented stud: captured students. That was many years ago—long before Oliver moved into the building. The apartment appeared to be gaudier now, Nicholas thought, unsure how that could be possible. Juan Diego did not pay attention to the décor. He had been too focused on getting Nicholas to love him again.

    Nicholas knew that having sex with Juan Diego was the only way to distract him from hurting Oliver. Years ago, Nicholas committed, only to himself, to sleep with no one other than Oliver, but that was proving difficult, especially as he continued to lure men in for the kill. He told himself that sex with his victims did not count; it did not violate his commitment to Oliver, but he knew that was a lie. He liked having sex, and he enjoyed killing people. He just needed to come to terms with balancing these passions with his love for Oliver. This was something he had been struggling with since he and Oliver went in search of Adam's family in Vermont many years ago.

Nicholas helped Juan Diego peel their clothes off, leaving a trail from the foyer. Naked, vulnerable and horny, Nicholas grabbed Juan Diego's hand and pulled him close. He wanted to get this over with so he could get to Oliver. Juan Diego kissed Nicholas. It was their first time together since London, and it felt like their first time at summer camp. Nicholas forgot how intoxicating Juan Diego tasted.

Juan Diego was a drug that Nicholas thought he had been cleansed of many years ago, but like any good junkie, Nicholas took one taste of Juan Diego, and he was transported back to the blissful wonder of their youth together. The two rolled around under the sheets, sharing and shooting fluids before finally collapsing on their backs, sweaty, exhausted, and satisfied. Within minutes, Juan Diego was asleep.

The drug started wearing off almost immediately as Nicholas lay quietly beside Juan Diego. He could feel the dopamine fading away as reality came back into focus. Nicholas was suddenly very angry with himself for sleeping with Juan Diego. He enjoyed the sex but knew it was wrong. Nicholas knew that when Juan Diego woke up, he would want more. He knew Juan Diego well enough to know that Juan Diego would think they were dating again, but that was not what Nicholas wanted. He wanted to get back to Oliver, to be with Oliver.

* * * * *

Several police officers searched the building for a man in a delivery uniform. The doorman called them as Nicholas instructed but could not tell them much since Nicholas had been vague. The first two officers to arrive listened to what the doorman had to say before they went up to see Oliver. The doorman called up to Oliver letting him know the officers were heading his way. Oliver was happy to know that the police were in his building, but he was furious that Nicholas had disappeared, again.

Even though Nicholas instructed Oliver not to open the door, knowing the police were in the building gave Oliver comfort enough to lower his guard. When he answered his door and saw two young officers standing before him looking annoyed, Oliver wanted to spit everything out. He wanted to tell the police about Nicolas, Redwood Manor, and Juan Diego, about everything, but he stood silent. He contemplated what he would say, what consequences his words could have, or the ripple effect they might cause.

"Mr. McPherson," one officer said. "We understand from your doorman that you are in danger. That someone is trying to hurt you or maybe even kill you."

Oliver looked at the two officers. This was his chance. This was the moment he had been waiting for, wanting. He could help himself, or he could help Nicholas; maybe they were the same thing. He was having trouble distinguishing between the two anymore.

"Yes," Oliver said.

"Can you elaborate," asked the second officer.

"Yes," Oliver said.

"A little more than that," the first chimed in.

"Sorry," Oliver said. "There is a man named Juan Diego, or at least that is the name he gave me back in California. He has been stalking me for a few months, maybe longer. I received a tip that he was in the building."

"Stalking you for months?" the first officer asked. "Have you filed any complaints?"

"No," Oliver replied.

The officers looked at each other, then back at Oliver. They wore a look as if to tell Oliver that he needed to be more verbose.

"He said he would kill me and my friends if I alerted the police," Oliver continued. Nicholas was rubbing off on him.

"And have you seen this Juan Diego person in the building today?" the second officer asked.

"No, but I got a call that he had entered the building an hour ago."

"By who?" the first officer asked.

"Who what?" Oliver asked.

The officer looked at Oliver with a perplexed look.

"Oh, you mean, by whom," Oliver laughed, mocking the officer.

"Mr. McPherson, this is not a joking matter," said the second officer. "If someone is in the building trying to kill you, you need to take this more seriously."

The first officer spoke into the walkie-talkie on his shoulder, asking for immediate backup. Even if Oliver appeared to not want to take the matter seriously, the officer and his partner would follow protocol.

* * * * *

Nicholas was admiring the naked brown skin lying next to him. He ran his fingers over Juan Diego's shoulder and down his arm. Juan Diego was half asleep now, mainly in a state of ecstasy. As Nicholas moved his finger down Juan Diego's body, it reacted, growing to salute Nicholas. Juan Diego hoped Nicholas would grab him to continue their fun, but he did not. Instead, Nicholas slid out of bed and headed to the bathroom to clean up. It was time to say no to this drug, for good.

While Nicholas was in the shower, Juan Diego lay on the bed, soaking up the moment, rubbing his sticky stomach after finishing what Nicholas would not. He contemplated joining Nicholas in the shower. He wanted to be sure Nicholas was not going to run away again. He wanted to believe that Nicholas was telling the truth about getting out of the building together. By the time Nicholas came out of the bathroom, Juan Diego had fallen asleep again. He was exhausted from running, chasing, and having sex with his crush.

Once Nicholas was dressed, he looked out the living room window and saw the collection of police cars blocking traffic on the street below. He knew that he needed to be careful about his next steps. He could hear Juan Diego snoring quite loudly in the bedroom. He did not remember if Juan Diego snored years ago. He was loud.

This was the perfect opportunity to hand Juan Diego over to the police, thought Nicholas as he listened to what sounded like rocks in a blender. Nicholas walked out the front door of William's apartment and took the elevator to the lobby. An officer was standing by the door when it opened.

"Hello, officer," Nicholas said, panting to give the illusion that he had been running, rushing to be saved. "A stranger is hiding in my apartment."

"Come again," the officer said, confused by Nicholas' comment.

"Some man just forced his way into my apartment," Nicholas lied. "There was a struggle, but I was able to knock him out. He is in my apartment right now."

"So why did you come to the lobby?" the officer asked.

"I saw all the police cars outside, so I knew you would be down here. It was faster than calling 9-1-1," Nicholas said, annoyed that he had to explain so much detail. He was worried that Juan Diego would wake up and realize Nicholas was gone.

The officer signaled to another officer, and they headed up to apartment 1015. Nicholas told them the door was unlocked and that he would stay in the lobby for his safety. They bought the lies, but then they always did. Nicholas was good at making a lie seem like the truth. As the two officers exited the elevator, they saw Juan Diego leaving the apartment. The three looked at each other momentarily before Juan Diego ran towards the stairwell. The officers went chasing after him, yelling into their shoulders for help. The officers visiting with Oliver heard the call and left Oliver to help their colleagues, leaving Oliver exposed and vulnerable. With all the commotion, Nicholas slipped out the front door of Oliver's building and headed back to the coffee shop. On his way, he called Oliver.

"I have the police arresting Juan Diego right now," Nicholas sang into the phone, proud of his lucky escape. "Now is your time to leave. Meet me at the place of our first real date." Nicholas never waited for Oliver to say 'hello' or acknowledge the instructions. He was right back to his shenanigans again, not listening to Oliver, but doing what he believed was in the best interest of Oliver.

Oliver contemplated Nicholas' words. He was furious that Nicholas was continuing to treat Oliver like a child, like something Nicholas had to protect at all costs without consulting Oliver. He thought about calling Nicholas back and telling him to fuck off, to tell him that he was done, but he knew that would be a lie. He missed Nicholas. Juan Diego might have been Nicholas' drug of choice at one time, but now Nicholas was Oliver's addiction.

By the time Oliver reached his lobby, the police had captured Juan Diego. They had cuffed him in the stairwell between floors one and two and walked him through the lobby as Oliver walked out to meet Nicholas.

"He did this to me, Oliver," Juan Diego yelled. "Nicholas is only looking out for himself. Don't let him fool you."

"Shut up," one officer said to Juan Diego.

"Ask him about Elizabeth," Juan Diego shouted.

"Stop," Oliver yelled to the officers. "What did you just say?"

"You heard me," Juan Diego spat back at Oliver. "Your boy is not Saint Nicholas. He killed your cousin Elizabeth. He did it to prove his love for me."

"I said shut up," the officer yelled at Juan Diego. Then he and his partner pulled Juan Diego out of the building and put him in the back of a police car parked at the entrance, holding up traffic.

"Wait," Oliver yelled, chasing after the officers. "I need to know what he is talking about."

"Don't believe anything coming out of this man's mouth,

son," one of the older officers told Oliver, holding him from getting too close to the patrol car. "Thugs always start spouting lies as they are taken in. They are trying to redirect our attention."

Oliver was not buying the officer's answer. He did not want to give Juan Diego's words credit or validity, but at the same time, Oliver was not brushing them off either. He knew enough about Nicholas' past to know that Nicholas could do what Juan Diego was spewing into the air. The question for Oliver was deciding who he should believe; who he could believe more.

He watched the police car drive off with Juan Diego in the back seat. Juan Diego looked out through the barred window, trying to look back at Oliver. With the car out of sight, Oliver turned and started walking towards the train station. He could not believe he was heading back to Greenwich again.

Chapter Nineteen

Nicholas watched Oliver walk away. He thought about yelling out to him, but there were still too many police officers lingering around the building, and he did not want to draw any attention to himself. Instead, he sat by the window of the coffee shop like he had so many times before and watched Oliver walk away slowly, almost defeated.

While Nicholas was cleared of some crimes by the New York City police, he and Lawrence knew that Nicholas was not in the clear yet. The Vermont, Connecticut, and New York police departments each have separate murder cases they were separately trying to pin on Nicholas. Lawrence and Nicholas did not know yet that the FBI had opened their own investigation, and that Agent Dalrymple was getting closer to Nicholas — he had been called in by each of the three states and noticed some similarities among the cases.

* * * * *

As much as he wished he could have spent more time with Calvin, Eddie knew that they both had jobs to do. Rather than be upset about their time apart, he focused on their time together, which seemed to be less and less lately with the growing number of murder cases surfacing across the country.

Eddie stood in the center of his study. Today, the room is cluttered with a dozen easels, each holding large boards — one for each case—images of bloody bodies and evidence providing the violent aura of the room. Looking around the room, Eddie remembered a time when the study was bigger. He was smaller then, and there were no easels. This room was where his father spent endless days and nights yelling into the phone that still sat on the large mahogany desk at the far end of the room. That was long ago. Now, his dad sat in an urn, nothing more than ashes, on one of the many bookshelves that lined the room.

Holding a hot cup of tea in both hands, Eddie felt the room spin as he turned from easel to easel, looking for the connection between his cases. He knew it was there; he knew there had to be one. As he did, he wondered if Calvin was having as much trouble with his case. It had been weeks since he held Calvin in his arms, and now the large apartment felt even larger, empty without Calvin. Eddie needed Calvin. He could always see his cases differently when he was in Calvin's arms.

Eddie and Calvin met at the Farm during basic training. Back then, Eddie's dad was still alive but was already on his way to the urn, spending more and more time in the hospital, wishing his only child would give up his dream of working for the FBI. Eddie's family was old money from his mother's side. She always loved her son in ways her husband never could. She accepted Eddie for who he was, who he wanted to be, but her husband wanted more for his son. He wanted a wife for his son. Eddie hid the money part of his life almost more than he hid his sexuality. With Calvin, Eddie could be himself. Calvin did not care that Eddie was wealthy beyond his imagination. He only cared that Eddie loved him as much as he loved Eddie.

The two arrived at the Farm single and alone, and they quickly found themselves together and happy, but only in private. A year after graduation, Calvin traveled to New York and moved in with Eddie. Eddie's father was on the shelf in the study by then, his urn next to the one that held Eddie's mother. With his parents gone, the already big apartment felt enormous and empty. Even when they were alive, it still felt lonely. When Calvin moved in, the apartment was busy again. It has felt like a home for over a decade now: warm and loving. Their two Weimaraners, Princess, and Barnaby, completed their gay Normal Rockwell image.

Eddie knew in his gut that his cases were connected and was close to pinning them on one person. The boards had the whole story, but they weren't sharing it with Eddie yet. He had to look harder. He needed to see beyond the images in front of him. This was his specialty: finding the killer in the details that others overlooked. It was what he did best. It was one of the many characteristics Calvin loved about Eddie.

Images of Oliver and Nicholas were scattered across some of the boards, but not all. Eddie put down his tea and picked up a folder filled with transcripts of texts between the two, wondering if the police had been looking at them both from the wrong perspective. Before he could finish his thought, it was interrupted by the phone on the desk ringing.

* * * * *

Thirty minutes later, all the activity around Oliver's apartment had subsided. It was quiet again, by New York standards. Nicholas took that as his cue to get to Greenwich quickly. He did not want Oliver waiting at the King & Queen any longer than necessary for fear that Oliver would leave again.

Oliver arrived at the King & Queen long before Nicholas, even though he made one stop before getting on the train in New York. When Nicholas arrived, Oliver was sitting on a bench outside the restaurant. Nicholas was already apologizing as he stepped out of the cab.

"I am so sorry that ..." Nicholas started.

"Save it!" Oliver yelled back, interrupting Nicholas. "I am done with the games. And I mean it this time."

"I just saved your fucking life," Nicholas said before he could filter his response.

"No," Oliver yelled. "You stopped a guy from supposedly killing me. A man who never would have tried to kill me if you had not pulled me into your chaotic life."

"Babe," Nicholas said, regaining his composure and tone as he sat beside Oliver. "Let me start again.

"I never expected Juan Diego to resurface, so I never assumed you were in danger. And, as soon as I realized what was going on, I took the necessary action to protect you. He is in police custody now, right?"

"Yes," Oliver said, almost whispering.

"That means you are safe," Nicholas continued. "And with me again, finally. Hasn't this been our goal for what seems like forever now?"

"Yes," Oliver said again, looking at the ground.

The two were silent for longer than they wanted to be. Oliver was still angry with Nicholas but felt guilty for what was about to happen. He feared making eye contact with Nicholas for fear of changing his mind. Nicholas put his hand on Oliver's hand like he had so many years earlier when they first met on a park bench. Nicholas was relieved when Oliver did not pull away.

"Listen," Nicholas started. "I cannot stay. You know that, right?"

"No," Oliver said, tightening his grip on Nicholas' hand. "So, what's next?"

"Redwood Manor was supposed to be our sanctuary," Nicholas said. "I was hoping to stop running once we were both there."

"Yeah, well, that plan has been destroyed," Oliver said as he started to cry. "And I fear that our relationship is on a similar path. I am exhausted."

"Yes, Redwood Manor has burned to the ground, but we can start again. Come with me to Scotland," Nicholas said. "Let's finally run away… together."

"Burned to the ground?" Oliver asked.

"Yes, Juan Diego went there looking for you," Nicholas confessed. "When neither of us was there, George and his mother were killed, and then Juan Diego torched the place."

"That is the kind of life I am tired of living," Oliver said. "I am not interested in being at the center of a Hollywood action movie. I am done."

Oliver held Nicholas's hand tighter as tears ran down his face. Some of the tears were for the pain Nicholas had caused him over the years, and some were for what was about to happen. Before either of them could make another move or say another word, they were surrounded by police officers. Nicholas was so focused on Oliver that he did not see the undercover officers around them, watching, waiting. Two officers grabbed Nicholas off the bench, pulling his hand out of Oliver's.

"What did you do?" Nicholas yelled to Oliver as the officers forced him to the ground. "What did you do?"

"I am sorry," Oliver said through tears.

Chapter Twenty

Seagulls squawked overhead as the ocean slammed waves gently into the sand. The sounds were welcoming and soothing to Oliver. It had been a month since Juan Diego and Nicholas were arrested, and Oliver was still struggling with whether he had made the right decision about turning Nicholas in. Lawrence called Oliver several times during the first week, trying to create a timeline of events to make a case for Nicholas' freedom. Oliver cooperated, making it abundantly clear to Lawrence that he was exhausted.

As he answered Lawrence's questions, Oliver began to think about all the losses: Elizabeth, Howard, Camilla, Miles, Reed, Hunter, the list felt infinite. He wondered how one guy could suffer through so much loss and still be normal, still function. Maybe he wasn't normal, he thought. The question that kept surfacing for Oliver was whether all this death was because of him or Nicholas. He knew he was not directly responsible for the deaths, but the more Oliver thought about it, the more he felt partially responsible. He wondered if he could have prevented any of them and if many of them were killed because of Nicholas. He had not thought any of them were killed by Nicholas. Oliver was still struggling with what Juan Diego said as he was hauled away: Nicholas killed Elizabeth.

One truth that Oliver had come to terms with these last few weeks was that he still loved Nicholas. Any outsider would scratch their head as to how or why Oliver could still love Nicholas, could have ever loved Nicholas. But Oliver had accepted that truth:

through it all, he did love Nicholas. As Oliver sat in the warm sand, watching the sun being swallowed up by the vast, dark ocean, he wondered if this was how battered wives felt. He loved Nicholas and was happy to be out of the chaos, but that did not change the fact that he missed Nicholas every day.

Oliver watched a crab scuttle over the sand in search of dinner as a seagull swooped down and scooped it up. The crab never saw the gull's shadow move across the sand and never had a chance to escape. Oliver had escaped but now was wondering if it was what he wanted. He had begun second-guessing his decision to turn Nicholas. His thoughts were interrupted by the buzzing of his phone.

"Hello," Oliver said into his phone as he continued to push his toes through the soothing sand.

"Hi, Oliver," Lawrence responded. "I have some good news and some bad news."

"Good and bad for whom?" Oliver asked.

"Ultimately, you," Lawrence replied. He paused a bit longer than Oliver wanted before continuing with his news. "Nicholas is free. Everything the Connecticut police have on him is circumstantial. As much as they want to pin several murders on him, they do not have enough evidence to detain him any longer than they have. He is being released tomorrow morning."

"Is that the good news or the bad news?" Oliver asked sarcastically. He was wearing a massive smile as he asked the question. He wanted nothing more at that moment than to be in Nicholas' arms, but at the same time, he wanted nothing to do with Nicholas. He continued to be torn, struggling with his love or dependence on Nicholas. This news would force Oliver to make some hard decisions sooner than he thought he would have to.

"For you and Nicholas," Lawrence said. "It is great news. You two can finally be together, assuming that is what you still want."

Even though he had been contemplating life without Nicholas, hearing Lawrence say those words stung Oliver a little. The reality was setting in fast, and whether he liked it or not, the time to decide had come.

"So what is the bad news?" Oliver asked.

"The bad news is that Juan Diego has already been released."

"What?" Oliver yelled, jumping up quickly, scaring a flock of seagulls.

"It turns out that he was released several days ago. Much like Nicholas' case, there was no evidence to detain him. And with you not coming forward, the police had no reason to keep him locked up," Lawrence continued. "I am sorry, Oliver."

"He is going to find me again, isn't he?" Oliver asked.

"Yes, we have to assume you are still in danger," Lawrence replied. "I think you and Nicholas need to get out of town; go somewhere far away. And stay there."

"I don't want to keep playing these games," Oliver said. "I am tired of running. I want a normal life again."

"I want the same thing for you. Are you home?" Lawrence asked. "I can send a car around. It would be best if you stayed with me tonight. Tomorrow, we can pick up Nicholas together, and then I can put you both on a plane to somewhere safe."

The pros and cons list that Oliver had been formulating in his head lately around the idea of staying with Nicholas was beginning to tilt more towards the con side with the revelation that Juan Diego was still out there. Oliver believed that if Juan Diego was in New York and had been in California, he had to know about Martha's Vineyard. He would not be surprised if Juan Diego knew everything about him by now.

"No!" Oliver yelled into the phone. "You can get Nicholas and take him to Martha's Vineyard in three days. I will meet you both there to figure out the next steps. We are going to start doing things my way for a change."

Oliver hung up the phone before Lawrence could respond. As tired as he was, Oliver was finally ready to take control of his life situation. Battered or not, he loved Nicholas, but before he could live with him and grow old together, he needed to stop Juan Diego from hurting him or anyone else again.

Chapter Twenty-One

Nicholas was holed up in a motel on the outskirts of Woods Hole for a week. He was supposed to meet Oliver on Martha's Vineyard days ago, but severe weather shut down all ferries to and from the island, making Nicholas a prisoner in the drug-den of a motel. When Lawrence dropped Nicholas off at the motel, he made it abundantly clear to Nicholas how important it was for him and Oliver to leave the country, to go somewhere Juan Diego could never find them. Nicholas agreed. He had his mind set on Scotland and hoped Oliver would join him.

Alone in the motel room, Nicholas called Oliver multiple times but never got a response. He left many voicemails explaining that he was trying to get to the island; Nicholas assumed Oliver was waiting for him on Martha's Vineyard. What Nicholas did not know, could not know was that Oliver left Martha's Vineyard the day Lawrence told him that Nicholas and Juan Diego were released.

While trapped in the room, Nicholas contemplated his future, one he hoped still included Oliver. He was trying to figure out where Juan Diego would go next and what his next move might be. Nicholas knew that Juan Diego would not stop until Oliver was out of Nicholas' life forever. He now believed that turning Juan Diego over to the police was a mistake. He should have killed Juan Diego in William's apartment or, better yet, when they reconnected in London, he thought.

Now Nicholas lay alone in a strange bed in a dimly lit room, longing for the comfort of Oliver's embrace. A stench of sex and cigarettes filled the room. Little "no smoking" stickers were all over the room, walls, and furniture, but that did not stop previous occupants from smoking. Nicholas could almost see a stale cigarette haze floating in the air. He could taste it in his mouth and smell it on his clothes. He had to open the door to let some fresh air in, to let the storm in.

Standing outside his room, Nicholas leaned against a railing and looked down at the prominent center patio below. Everything was wet. The sky was dark. The two-story motel was square-shaped, with the center hollowed out to make room for a pool and roofless community space. Nicholas could see that many of the rooms lit up, and he was intrigued by the number of people coming and going in this weather.

Nicholas watched all the activity below for some time before noticing someone watching him. He was the guest, after all, in a motel whose residents treated it more like a drug-filled brothel than a motel. He watched two men on the patio below, near the pool, make an exchange under a small umbrella. Nicholas assumed it was a drug sale. Then he watched two girls wearing bikinis, or maybe it was underwear. It was hard to tell and probably did not matter. They came out of a room whose door opened to the pool patio. A cloud of marijuana smoke followed them.

Within minutes, the girls were soaked from the rain before being swallowed by the murky pool water. When they both emerged from the pool, neither was wearing a top. After splashing around in the water for a few minutes, they got out of the pool, cuddled together on a lounge chair and started making out. Nicholas watched in awe. He was not interested in seeing two girls make out, but he was surprised that two girls were naked, making out poolside during a rainstorm. He was confident they had to be strung out on some cocktail, probably unaware that it was raining.

When he looked back up to his floor, Nicholas noticed a man standing on the other side of the walkway, almost opposite him. The man was also leaning on the railing and watching the girls below. Nicholas watched the man looking at the girls before the man looked up and over at Nicholas. Seconds later, the man started walking. Nicholas thought he was walking away, but after another minute, the man was standing next to Nicholas. From afar, it was hard to see the man's appearance, so Nicholas was relieved that it was not Juan Diego. He was not ready to deal with him just yet.

"You like what you see?" The guy asked Nicholas.

"Before me or below me?" Nicholas asked back, wanting to be sure he understood the man's question. It had been weeks since he held a man, and while trying to hold out for Oliver, Nicholas was confident that the man was propositioning him.

"Either, really," the man responded. "I can get you anything you want. My name is Drew."

"What if I want you, Drew?" Nicholas asked, chuckling.

Drew was short and athletic. He was wearing shorts, flip-flops, and a tank top, which Nicholas thought odd, given all the rain. Drew was too skinny to wear a tank top, Nicholas thought. He had some muscle but not much, and his stringy arms were covered in tattoos. He spoke in a thick Boston accent. Nicholas looked Drew up and down, deciding that he was not fuckable.

"For the right price, you can have anything you want," Drew answered. "But I have to warn you…" he started to say.

"Let me stop you right there," Nicholas interrupted. "You are not my type. Neither are they." He pointed to the girls below, still making out in the rain.

Drew looked into Nicholas' bright green eyes, and that is when Nicholas saw rage looking back at him.

"I am everyone's type," Drew said, almost whispering since he was close to Nicholas' face. He grabbed Nicholas's crotch and squeezed tightly. "You can pay me $100 to let go, or I will squeeze so tight you pass out. Then I will take all your money."

Nicholas contemplated his next move carefully. He knew Drew was an amateur, some junkie who thought he was much cooler than he was. Nicholas knew the type all too well.

"That is my room right here," Nicholas said, nodding to the right. "Let's go inside and have some fun. I like it rough, and apparently so do you."

Drew was not expecting Nicholas' response. Every other time Drew pulled this stunt, his victim paid up and moved on. Drew squeezed tighter, but Nicholas did not react, so he let go and followed Nicholas into the room, slightly defeated. Once Nicholas closed the door, he turned around and punched Drew in the throat. Drew grabbed his neck and gasped for air. While he struggled to breathe, Nicholas lectured him.

"I should have warned you that people don't usually threaten me and live to talk about it," Nicholas started. "I don't care who you are or how small your dick must be for you to be such a bully. And I cannot believe that bullshit line works on anyone.

"I am in this shit hole of a motel trying to save my relationship, to be with the man of my dreams, and no one will stand in the way. Not you. Not Juan Diego. Not anyone.

"You will survive. I mean you will live. Your ego will surely be bruised, and if I hear about this little incident from anyone, I will hunt you and your family down, and then I will kill each of them in front of you before killing you. Do you understand what I am saying?"

Drew nodded 'yes' as he continued to catch his breath.

"Great," Nicholas replied. "Take off all your clothes. I will not ask twice."

Once naked, Drew stood, cupping his crotch.

"Now go lay on that bed," Nicholas demanded, pointing to the bed farthest from the door.

Once Drew was flat on the bed, Nicholas tore the pillowcases apart and tied Drew's hands and feet to parts of the bed. Drew tried to fight Nicholas off, but Nicholas knew where to punch each time. First was the throat. Second was the balls. Drew was not ready to learn what would get hit next, so he stopped fighting and became completely submissive to Nicholas' demands.

Completely secured to the bed, Drew was helpless. He tried to free himself once Nicholas stepped away from the bed, but the knots were tight. Nicholas picked Drew's shorts up off the floor to see what he might have in his pockets. Nichols found a syringe, a roll of cash, and a joint.

"What do we have here?" Nicholas asked as he waved the syringe above Drew's head. "And don't lie to me."

"It is a cocktail. You should try it. You might like it," Drew said, trying to hold back tears.

Irritated with Drew's flippant attitude, Nicholas grabbed Drew's dick, pulled back the foreskin, and injected the syringe into Drew's meatus. Nicholas did not let go until the entire syringe had been emptied. Drew screamed.

Drew tried to wiggle free from Nicholas' grip but could not. The rush of the cocktail ran through his blood system almost too fast. His entire body started shaking. He shat in the bed, then got hard. His lips started turning blue. Nicholas pulled the needle out of Drew's dick and stepped back.

Of all the cocktails Nicholas had created to subdue his victims, none worked as wildly or quickly as what Drew brought to this party. He watched Drew's body quiver and then go still. It continued to shit, the brown liquid quickly spreading across the bed. The smell of old cigarettes was finally covered up by something more disgusting. Minutes later, Drew vomited. It shot up into the air a few inches before landing all over his face, with much of it seeping back into his mouth, choking him. Seconds later, Drew's entire body stopped moving.

Looking at Drew's dead body, Nicholas felt utterly unsatisfied. He had not intended to kill Drew. Being able to kill Drew was a pleasant surprise, but Nicholas felt nothing from it. When Nicholas would kill, he liked how it made him feel. He would often get off, but this time, he felt empty, unfinished. Nicholas sat on the clean bed, looking at Drew's vomit-covered blue limps. The smell was revolting.

Nicholas knew he could not stay in his motel room for another minute. The stench was too much. He grabbed the money and joint off the bed stand and walked out of the room, closing the door behind him. It was too wet outside to find another motel, so he walked along the balcony to another room. He picked the lock and stepped inside. It was late, and he felt confident that no one would be renting this room tonight. As he closed the door behind him and locked it, he noticed how much nicer this room was and how much cleaner it smelled. Exhausted, Nicholas stripped off his clothes and collapsed on the bed closest to the door. He needed to sleep.

Chapter Twenty-Two

Juan Diego sat in the same coffee shop Nicholas frequented so often when he watched Oliver, looking out the window towards Oliver's building. He was watching, waiting to get a glimpse of Oliver. Juan Diego knew Oliver was home. He had seen Oliver's lights turning on and off over the last few days. Nicholas should have been his priority; he usually was, but after the stunt Nicholas pulled recently, Juan Diego decided to refocus his energy.

Being captured by the New York police certainly slowed his efforts to have Nicholas all to himself but leaving his fingerprints and mugshot with the police infuriated Juan Diego. He knew he needed to take extra precautions for a little while. The last thing Juan Diego wanted was to have his mug shot make its way to San Francisco.

The idea of walking into Oliver's building was out of the question. Juan Diego knew the doorman would recognize him and call the police again, so he sat in the coffee shop waiting for Oliver to leave his apartment. Juan Diego could be unapologetically patient when stalking his victims. In this case, he was so focused on watching for Oliver that he did not realize Oliver was also watching him. Oliver returned from Martha's Vineyard with one mission: to lure Juan Diego out of hiding.

Oliver took a page from the Nicholas playbook and placed a small video camera on a shelf in the coffee shop. Oliver watched the coffee shop activity on his phone from the comfort of his apartment, patiently watching Juan Diego. He watched Juan Diego come and go for two days. Where Juan Diego went when not sitting in the coffee shop remained a mystery to Oliver, but it was one he was less concerned about. So long as Oliver was able to get Juan Diego to follow him when he was ready to be followed was all Oliver cared about. He had devised a plan to stop Juan Diego from bothering him or Nicholas for good.

On the third day of watching Juan Diego, Oliver decided to make his move, to put his plan into action. When he saw Juan Diego sitting in the coffee shop, Oliver knew it was time. As Oliver looked out the window, he could see that it was raining; the edge of the storm currently tormenting Nicholas was keeping New York under dark clouds.

Nicer weather would have been his preference, but Oliver knew that today had to be the day when he confronted Juan Diego. Oliver walked out the front door of his building and lingered for a few minutes under his awning, taunting Juan Diego to come out and follow. Oliver did not want to look toward the coffee shop or let Juan Diego know he was being watched. Instead, after a few minutes of pretending to fidget with his phone, Oliver opened an umbrella; the vibrant rainbow stripes were a beacon of brightness on an otherwise wet and gloomy day. This circular rainbow stood out among the crowd of black umbrellas, which was part of Oliver's plan. He wanted Juan Diego to follow him and not get lost along the busy sidewalks of New York.

After several more minutes of standing around with the opened umbrella, Oliver started his hike toward Central Park. Excited to finally see Oliver, Juan Diego jumped up and ran out of the coffee shop, looking around to ensure no police officers were patrolling. His short time with the New York police was unpleasant, and he wanted to be careful not to cross their path again anytime soon. Being questioned about Oliver was the least of his concerns since he knew the San Francisco police were looking for him. They hadn't yet put a nationwide alert out for Juan Diego, at least not that he was aware of. He feared that if he were caught again, he could be extradited to the West Coast and never again get the chance he believed he had now as he went after Oliver in the rain.

Juan Diego was so rushed to catch Oliver that he left his umbrella in the coffee shop. He was getting soaked as he tried to keep up with Oliver's pace. Passersby, protected by raincoats and umbrellas, looked at Juan Diego as he continued to march towards Oliver, seemingly unphased by how wet he was becoming. He had one mission: not to lose the rainbow umbrella.

Oliver would stop and pretend to admire a shop window every so often to make sure that Juan Diego was still following him. After all his planning, he was not about to lose Juan Diego because of the rain. Eventually, they both made it into Central Park. Because of the depressingly dreary weather, the park was quite empty. No food carts could be seen, and very few people were out, precisely the scene Oliver wanted. As Oliver moved further into the park, with Juan Diego quickly gaining ground on him, the intensity of the rain strengthened. The storm was getting stronger. Even the large, bright umbrella that had protected Oliver so far on this journey was beginning to struggle to keep him dry. Every so often, the wind would swoop under and try to pull the umbrella out of Oliver's hand, getting Oliver very wet. Oliver held on to the umbrella tightly. He was not about to lose it, lose Juan Diego.

Once Oliver reached the middle of Bow Bridge, he stopped. He had been to this point many times before, always in better weather and often with Nicholas. He turned around but could not see Juan Diego. He was hopeful that he had not lost Juan Diego in the final stretch of his plan. As he watched, waiting, Oliver thought about Nicholas and their first kiss on this bridge. He thought about their very first kiss and all their good times since. He was sure he was crying, but his face was too wet to know. When he looked up, he saw Juan Diego standing just a few yards away.

"He doesn't love you," Juan Diego yelled, trying to be heard above the whistling wind. "He is incapable of loving anyone, even me. I see that now."

"You cannot hurt me," Oliver yelled back. "Your words have no power over me. It is *YOU* that he does not love. I know he loves me." Oliver said as he poked his chest to emphasize his words.

"Stop fooling yourself, Oliver," Juan Diego said as he stepped closer. "You and he are too different: good and evil, oil and water. You just don't go together. He and I, on the other hand, well, we are carved from the same stone."

"You can think what you want," Oliver said. "But the truth is, he will only ever see one of us again."

Juan Diego took a few more steps to get closer to Oliver. They were no longer standing at a yelling distance from each other. They could each see the darkness of the other's eyes. Juan Diego thought he saw fear in Oliver's eyes. Juan Diego was there to kill Oliver. He was prepared to take Oliver's life right there on the bridge. He was so consumed with hate for Oliver and love for Nicholas that he did not care if anyone saw him now as he lunged forward to hit Oliver.

As Juan Diego leaped, fist forward, he was unprepared for the sharp pain that pierced his chest. In his apartment, Oliver fastened a switchblade to the tip of his umbrella, a makeshift tool he had spent many hours assembling. It might have been more noticeable if the rain had not been so intense and the sky so dark. As Juan Diego dove for Oliver, hoping to punch his face, Oliver quickly flung open his umbrella, separating him and Juan Diego with a bright rainbow in this dark moment. The blade struck Juan Diego in the heart, and Oliver pushed the umbrella toward Juan Diego to keep him from getting any closer. With each shove, Juan Diego let out a scream. He could not reach around the bright rainbow. He could not even see Oliver as he felt the blade plow deeper into his chest.

Oliver quickly pulled out, closing the umbrella. Juan Diego was spilling blood on the bridge and onto Oliver. The gash in his chest cried for him, staining his wet clothes. Juan Diego put both hands over his heart, trying to stop the bleeding, and when he did, Oliver dropped the umbrella and punched Juan Diego in the stomach. This second strike happened so fast. Juan Diego never had a chance to react and stop Oliver. He was losing blood too quickly and could not prevent his chest from leaking blood all over him. Oliver pulled Juan Diego in close, almost as if to hug him.

"It ends here," Oliver whispered into Juan Diego's ear. "You will never bother Nicholas nor me again. Do you hear me?"

Oliver held Juan Diego for a minute, distracting him from covering the large hole in his body. Oliver did not care that he was covered in Juan Diego's blood or that he might be leaving evidence on him. All Oliver cared about at that moment was killing Juan Diego. He never felt so empowered to hurt anyone, let alone kill them, as he did then. Once Oliver felt Juan Diego go limp, Oliver turned Juan Diego towards the railing and let go of him, pushing him over the side of the bridge. He watched Juan Diego's body fall into the Lake.

Oliver pulled the knife off the umbrella and threw the knife into the Lake. He opened the umbrella to let the rain wash away any blood. Nicholas would have scolded Oliver for the sloppy crime scene, but he did not care; Oliver was not thinking about the trail he was leaving behind. Oliver leaned on the railing, under the umbrella once again, and watched Juan Diego's body float for a few seconds before sinking, being swallowed up by the dark water. Oliver kept looking at where the water had swallowed Juan Diego's body, waiting for Juan Diego to resurface, but he never did. The rain continued to fall heavily, rinsing Oliver of Juan Diego's blood and washing the crime scene clean.

Standing against the railing, looking out across the Lake, Oliver could finally hear himself, feel himself crying. He was crying because he felt alone in that moment. He was crying because he had just done what he disliked the most about Nicholas, and it felt good.

Chapter Twenty-Three

The bright sun filled the room, softly waking Nicholas with a warm kiss. The warmth felt good against his naked body. He was dreaming of Oliver and of the last time they made love. It felt so real; the dream did.

As the sun took over more of the room, engulfing it with light, Nicholas and Oliver were one in Nicholas' dream. Their bodies were sweaty together, one penetrating the other. Nicholas was moaning as their two bodies moved to the rhythm of the other. Nicholas could see the smile on Oliver's face; he could feel his explosion running through him. At that moment, Nicholas was the happiest he had been in a long time, completely unaware that he was dreaming. Nicholas then saw Juan Diego standing above Oliver with a knife. Nicholas yelled and begged Juan Diego to stop, but it was too late. The new warmth Nicholas felt was his lover's blood painting his naked body, staining it forever. With one final scream, Nicholas woke as he shot into the air, into the sheets. He was soaking wet. He jumped up, forgetting for a moment where he was. He did not recognize the room and wondered where Oliver and Juan Diego had disappeared; the dream felt real. Nicholas looked around and realized he was alone.

Nicholas grabbed boxers off the floor and dried himself as he sat on the edge of the bed, trying to decide if his explosion was caused by the dream of having sex with Oliver or because the dream also included Juan Diego. Could he love them both? Nicholas wondered as he sniffed the sticky boxers before throwing them across the room. Then suddenly, as if jolted awake again, Nicholas realized it was sunny outside. The storm had passed, which meant he could get to the island. At that moment, Nicholas decided he could no longer ponder his dream's meaning. He needed to get to Oliver.

Rushing around the room, Nicholas pulled his jeans off the floor and pulled them over his legs, leaving his wet boxers for the maid. Today, he would be going commando, which is how he always preferred to be until Oliver changed his habit. Nicholas put his shirt on, buttoned it up, and then slipped into his old sneakers and hoodie. He did not care about showering. He wanted to get to Oliver as quickly as possible.

Nicholas looked at his disheveled appearance in the mirror above the television. He did not like the person looking back at him; he almost did not even recognize him — the reflection of an unshaven, tired man looking sad and defeated.

"What happened to you?" he quietly asked himself.

He used to have everything so well planned out, always in control. His obsession with Oliver was blinding him, or maybe it was Juan Diego causing him to make more mistakes and take less care of himself. Either way, he knew it needed to stop.

Nicholas smirked at the stranger in the mirror as if to say, 'fuck you,' before scanning the room to be sure he was not leaving anything incriminating behind. He was not coming back. Nicholas ran out the door towards the dock. As he moved along the balcony, he saw the collection of prostitutes and drug addicts strung out around the pool, wet and asleep. It looked like a murder scene he could have created or would be comfortable leaving behind, but these people were slowly killing themselves. Nicholas did not care. He was on the street within minutes, moving closer and closer to the ferry dock. He had one mission, the same mission he had had for months… get to Oliver and be with Oliver… forever.

On the ferry's top deck, Nicholas drank the salty air, almost bathing in it as the boat cut through the calm waters. Several police officers were walking around the ferry, patrolling but not looking for anyone. Nicholas saw them, and although he was not charged with any crimes in Massachusetts, he knew it was the Connecticut police who were still looking for him. After all, he had left quite a trail of dead bodies over the years and quite a mess with the explosion of the house he rented in Greenwich. Because Nicholas believed he was finally so close to being with Oliver again, he wanted to stay clear of anyone in a blue uniform, so he sat quietly with his hoodie covering much of his face.

By the time the boat docked, Nicholas was standing at the door, first in line, waiting for the crew to open it. Once they did, he ran down the ramp and jumped into the first taxi he found, and before he knew it, Nicholas was out of the cab and standing in front of Oliver's cottage. He had been here many times before, never with Oliver or with Oliver's knowledge, so he was nervous as he approached the front door. He knocked, but no one answered.

After a few minutes, Nicholas knocked again, and still no answer. The conversation with Lawrence was playing through his mind; he was supposed to meet Oliver at the cottage in three days. That was six days ago. Nicholas looked in some windows to what appeared to be an empty home, so he walked around the cottage to see if Oliver was out back or on the beach, but Oliver was nowhere in sight. Nicholas knocked on the back door, and still no response.

"Fuck!" Nicholas yelled louder than he intended.

"Can I help you?" a voice from the beach yelled back.

Nicholas turned to see an older gentleman standing a few yards from the house. The man looked to be in his mid-60s. He wore a sloppy head of grey hair, which bled into a black and white beard. His eyes were hidden behind cheap sunglasses. His tanned, almost leathery skin wrapped more muscle than most 60-year-old men wore. He was dressed in a tank top, shorts, and flip-flops and held a thick rope in one hand; at the other end was a spotted Great Dane who stood quietly, politely beside her owner.

"Sorry," Nicholas said. "This is my friend's cottage, and I was supposed to meet him here a few days ago, but the storm kept me away."

"Ah yes, that was a big one," the man replied. "The biggest we have seen around here in some time. But I am afraid you missed Oliver. He left before the storm."

"Wait, what?" Nicholas asked. "You know Oliver?"

"I live next door," the man said, pointing to a cottage some hundred yards away. "I knew his mother quite well; watched him grow up.

"I was boarding the front windows when I saw him get in a cab last week. I assumed he was getting off the island before he was trapped here like the rest of us.

"You must be Nicholas," the old man continued. "You are as handsome as he described."

"You know my name?" Nicholas asked, excited at the idea that Oliver talked about him.

"Let's just say that after a few whiskeys while watching the sunset a few times, Oliver unloaded on me," the man said. "Anyway, from what little I know, you need to go find him. He loves you."

"That is why I am here," Nicholas proclaimed. "I love him, too."

The two chit-chatted a little longer before Nicholas thanked the man and headed back toward town. He decided to walk; he did not have the time to wait for a taxi. He needed to get off the island and find Oliver. The old man and his dog watched Nicholas leave before returning to their walk along the beach, searching for what the storm might have brought ashore.

* * * * *

Oliver woke to his phone ringing. By the time he realized the source of the noise, it had stopped. He sat up in bed and looked around his room. He could see a pile of wet clothes on the bathroom floor, lines of red escaping the pile. He thought about what had happened, what he had done, and wondered if it had all been a dream. The pile indicated otherwise, and his hands were still shaking. Oliver could not believe that he had killed a man—killed Juan Diego. He was supposed to feel relieved; that is what he kept telling himself last night. Oliver was repeating those words now. But he was not relieved. He hated himself for taking the life of another person, not just any person, but a past lover of his boyfriend. Were they still boyfriends, he wondered as all these thoughts raced through his mind.

He needed to tell Nicholas; he wanted to tell him. But tell him what? Tell him that he lured Juan Diego and trapped him so that he could kill him. Tell him that he liked it; liked killing another human? Could he tell his serial killing boyfriend that he also liked to take people's lives? No, thought Oliver; this was a one-time thing. He kept telling himself that killing Juan Diego was a preemptive, self-defensive choice, not a premeditated plan to end a life. But it was premeditated and well-planned, and Oliver knew it.

As Oliver stepped out of bed, his phone started ringing again.

"Hello?"

"Hey, babe," Nicholas casually said as if it were just a regular call, not that they were talking for the first time since Oliver turned Nicholas over to the police.

"Hi."

"Where are you?" Nicholas asked with patience, even though he was angry that he had spent a week waiting to get to the island only to find Oliver gone. "More importantly, how are you?"

"Good. Better."

"Great," Nicholas said. "So, listen, I think we need to talk."

"Isn't that what we are doing right now?" Oliver asked.

"You know what I mean," Nicholas fired back, getting annoyed at Oliver's tone. "I don't blame you or hate you. I would've done the same thing the more I think about it. I have not been kind or fair to you, and I am truly sorry."

"Okay," Oliver said. He wanted to tell Nicholas that Juan Diego was dead but did not know how to start.

"I love you," Nicholas said, letting those words linger a moment before continuing. "I know I certainly do not deserve your love, not now. But I want to earn it back; I hope to earn it back. Your love gives me life, and yes, I know how stupid that might sound to you, especially now."

"Stop," Oliver interrupted. "I love you, too."

"Can we meet up?" Nicholas asked, excited to hear that Oliver still loved him.

"I am in my apartment," Oliver offered. "But I am not sure that meeting here is the safest place."

"I have been exonerated of all charges in New York," Nicholas offered with cocky excitement. "I don't have to keep running or hiding anymore. I am a free man, well almost." He knew he was lying again.

"If you say so."

"But I hear you," Nicholas said. "Let's go back to Vermont. I have some property up there. We can hide away again; reconnect and recommit to each other."

Oliver agreed to go with Nicholas to Vermont. He did not know Nicholas had property there and found it odd that Nicholas never mentioned it when they traveled through Vermont together, looking for information on Adam.

"Sure, but we need to drive together," Oliver insisted. "I cannot relive Redwood Manor again. You understand, right?

"Of course, babe," Nicholas said. "I completely understand."

"Great. Where are you?" Oliver asked, knowing that Nicholas was probably on Martha's Vineyard.

"I am at your cottage," Nicholas said. "Lawrence told me to meet you here. He said that you asked to have me meet you here."

"Yes. Sorry about that mix-up," Oliver lied. "Let's meet at the train station in New Haven. We can rent a car from there."

"New Haven might not be the best location!" Nicholas yelled unexpectedly. "Let's meet in Providence."

"Sure," Oliver replied, wanting to ask why New Haven was not a good place to meet. "See you there in about five hours."

By the time Oliver hung up the phone, he was crying again. He had accidentally stepped on the pile of bloody, wet clothes on the bathroom floor as he walked around talking with Nicholas. The reality of killing Juan Diego slapped him in the face again, and he was not sure how to keep this secret.

Oliver picked up the wet clothes and squeezed them in the sink before putting them into a trash bag, leaving the sink filled with pink water. Oliver opened his front door to see if the hallway was clear. It was. He walked ten feet to the trash shoot, almost tiptoeing, and dropped the heavy bag into the dark hole, listening to the plastic slide along the metal walls of the shoot. If Nicholas had been there, he would have scolded Oliver for breaking yet another cardinal rule of killing.

Back in his apartment, Oliver started making his morning cup of tea. He sat at the table as the water boiled, thinking about his life. He was thinking about Nicholas and trying to remember what Nicholas did to seduce Oliver the first time. Was it his eyes, Oliver wondered, or maybe his patience and kindness? Oliver could not remember, and it was bothering him. He proclaimed to Nicholas that he loved him but had lost track of why he loved him. The teapot whistled loudly, shaking Oliver out of his trance.

He poured the scolding water into the teacup, and while he let it seep, he looked up the train schedule to Providence. He agreed to meet Nicholas at the station around three, although he was suddenly having second thoughts about going. He wanted to; he felt he needed to, but he was worried about how he would tell Nicholas about Juan Diego.

Chapter Twenty-Four

The five-hour drive from Providence to Colchester was peaceful and breathtaking. Oliver took in the vibrant colors of death as Mother Nature began her colorful steps toward winter. Nicholas did all the driving and most of the talking, almost purposely filling the air with chatter to keep Oliver from asking any questions. Unprovoked, Nicholas was telling Oliver things he once thought would never pass through his lips. He was flawed, much like his biological father, Adam.

As much as he tried to paint a picture of perfection, especially around Oliver, Nicholas had concluded that all his years of lying, killing, and avoiding the truth had to end. As he rambled about different snippets of his past, Nicholas realized that he was speaking from the heart for the first time. He was talking naturally and honestly, not trying to spin a story or spew a headline to create an illusion of who he really was.

Nicholas' stories were disconnected, so to Oliver, the conversation felt like sound bites on the six o'clock news. The stories were memories Nicholas felt compelled to share with Oliver as they drove through the beautiful New England countryside. A few tears slid down Nicholas' face as he talked. They were tears of joy, of happiness... of honesty.

A few hours into the drive, Nicholas stopped rambling and reached over to grab Oliver's hand. It had been so long since the two had touched. Nicholas longed for the feel of Oliver's soft skin. Oliver did not pull away. He readjusted their hands so they were tightly locked together. Nicholas smiled.

"I am sorry," Oliver finally said. "For everything."

"Don't be silly," Nicholas said almost immediately. "I owe you an apology. I know that I have made your life a living hell for so long, which was never my intention. I am sorry for everything."

Nicholas was trying to lump the murder of all of Oliver's friends into that apology without spelling it all out for Oliver. Still, he did not think Oliver would understand the apology as he intended. This apology was all part of Nicholas' goal of coming clean to Oliver. At that moment, holding Oliver's hand, Nicholas did not think he would sing out a roll call of names. He was not ready to be that forthcoming this quickly, but he was satisfied with his general apology and believed that Oliver was, too.

Oliver squeezed Nicholas' hand.

"For as long as I can remember, all I wanted was to be with you," Nicholas said through tears. "I truly am sorry for the fiasco of Redwood Manor and for Juan Diego, for everything. I mean it."

With Nicholas sharing so much and appearing vulnerable, Oliver wanted to tell Nicholas about Juan Diego. Now seemed like the best time, the right time, but no words escaped each time he opened his mouth. He tried repeatedly, but each time, only air came out. He thought he could hear himself confessing to Nicholas, but he knew that was not true.

"I understand," Oliver finally said. "I want to be with you, too, but I need more honesty. I have enjoyed these last few hours. I feel like you are opening up and trusting me enough for you to show me the real you."

"I am trying," Nicholas said as he wiped his eyes dry.

"Tell me about the first person you killed," Oliver said, surprising Nicholas with his directness. "Not the person, but why did you do it, and how did it make you feel?"

"Babe, you do not want to hear that," Nicholas said. "I am trying not to focus on death anymore. I want to focus on life, on us."

"I understand," Oliver said. "But I want to know. I need to know everything. It will help me understand the true you even more; it will help me process everything."

Nicholas looked over to see Oliver staring back at him, smiling and tightening his grip on Nicholas' hand. Nicholas smiled back.

"I want to kiss you right now," Nicholas said.

Oliver let himself get pulled towards Nicholas, and they kissed.

"Now, put your eyes back on the road," Oliver said as he pulled back. "There will be much more of that once we get to the cabin. Stop procrastinating and tell me about the first time you killed someone."

"You make it sound so, I don't know... violent," Nicholas said.

"Was it?" Oliver asked. "Violent, I mean."

"It was not premeditated if that is what you mean," Nicholas lied.

"No?" Oliver asked.

The car slowed down and then turned onto a dirt road. The road was well-tended; it was wide and level and had a lot of gravel to keep it from becoming a muddy mess each Spring, which in

Vermont is more common than one might expect. Nicholas drove the car slowly along the road as they both took in the scenery around them, nature engulfing them, Mother Nature hugging them as they moved farther from the main road.

"Isn't nature so beautiful?" Nicholas asked, deflecting away from Oliver's question. "Look at all those colors and the bright sky. That blue is so clear."

"I am not going to let you avoid my question," Oliver said. "We can enjoy this spectacle around us now, but you will answer me... eventually."

Two miles later, they came upon a clearing, and a log cabin sat at the far end of that vast open space. Nicholas stopped the car as the road turned into lush green. The two sat silently for a moment, taking in the beautiful colors and vibrant brush surrounding them. A large buck jumped out from between two trees and stood a few yards in front of Nicholas and Oliver. The buck looked around momentarily, then galloped across the yard before disappearing into the trees on the far side of the clearing.

"This place is so beautiful," Oliver said, breaking the silence.

"I am glad you like it," Nicholas said. "We are sitting in the middle of 500 acres of solitude. Hopefully, we can call this place home."

"Home?" asked Oliver with a little laugh. "I only packed enough clothes for a few days."

"Remember Fiji?" Nicholas asked, laughing loudly. "Who needs clothes?"

"Fiji is a tropical island," Oliver fired back. "This is Vermont. We will freeze if we stay naked all the time."

"Not if we cuddle more," Nicholas laughed as he stepped out of the SUV, happy to have diverted Oliver away from the topic of his first kill. He was not prepared to tell Oliver about Toby. He knew that would open another book of questions, and the last thing Nicholas wanted while hiding out in the Vermont countryside was to be interrogated.

"I have no cell service," Oliver said as he spun around, holding his phone.

Nicholas grabbed the phone out of Oliver's hand.

"Sorry, but this place is off the grid," Nicholas said as he laughed.

"Not again," Oliver exclaimed.

"We do not need the outside world when we have each other, babe."

Oliver was not amused. He grabbed his phone back from Nicholas and pushed Nicholas away as he tried to kiss Oliver. Then Oliver walked across the clearing and up the stairs to the cabin porch. He sat on the swinging bench and looked out over the clearing, over Nicholas and their rented SUV. Oliver was taking in the isolation, and for a moment, it almost felt like how Redwood Manor should have been. At least this time, he had Nicholas with him.

Nicholas grabbed their bags from the back of the SUV. When he got to the porch, he dropped the bags and tapped a code on the keypad to open the front door. A few minutes later, Oliver followed. Inside, the cabin was much larger than it looked from the front. The high ceilings looked higher because the floor was below ground level. After walking into what Oliver considered a foyer, he took a few steps into a sunken space with an open living room, dining room, and kitchen combination that looked to take up much of the first floor. He could not see the hallway and four bedrooms that sat up and behind the open space. He looked up and saw wooden spiral stairs leading to what looked like a large loft.

"This place is huge," Oliver said without realizing he was speaking out loud.

"Yeah, probably too big for us," Nicholas said. "The upside is that we have space to move around. We will not be on top of each other all the time here."

"Who said that was a bad thing?" Oliver asked with a smirk.

"You know what I mean, babe," Nicholas said, laughing.

"So, is this your place?" Oliver asked.

"It is OUR place," Nicholas replied. Oliver looked across the room at Nicholas, raising his eyebrows as if to question Nicholas silently.

"The cabin belonged to Peter," Nicholas finally said. "He bought it when I was in middle school. We would come up here a few times a year to escape the big city."

"Since when is Greenwich a big city?" Oliver asked, laughing.

"Good point," Nicholas said. "Honestly, I forgot about this place. I have not been up here in years. Lawrence reminded me about it."

"I am going in search of the master bedroom," Oliver said as he picked up his suitcase.

"Straight down that hall," Nicholas said, pointing. "I am going to take inventory of our food supply."

"Our what?" Oliver asked as he dropped his bag and turned back towards Nicholas.

"Food," Nicholas said. "We forgot to stop and pick up food. There are only a few old cans of beans here and some peanut butter."

"How far away is the store?" Oliver asked.

"Maybe an hour away," Nicholas offered. "I honestly do not remember."

Nicholas could see Oliver's exhaustion and annoyance, first from the journey and now the news about their food situation.

"If you want to stay here, I can make a quick food run and be back in a couple of hours, tops," Nicholas said. "I mean, if you are exhausted and want to rest. I don't mind."

Oliver looked at Nicholas and studied his face to see if he was being tested. He did not want to go. The idea of more driving did not sound pleasant to Oliver, but at the same time, he was not sure he was ready to let Nicholas venture off on his own again. Oliver's first thought was that Nicholas would not come back. He hated himself for thinking that of Nicholas, but he felt justified, given Nicholas' history of disappearing.

"Do you mind if I stay behind?" Oliver finally asked. "I don't want you getting lost out there, and I hate you being out there by yourself, but I am beat."

"Not at all," Nicholas said. "You rest. I will be back before you know it."

Nicholas kissed Oliver, grabbed the rental keys off the table by the door, and was gone. Oliver was a little surprised at how quickly Nicholas bolted, but he chalked it up to Nicholas wanting to get out and back as soon as possible.

Chapter Twenty- Five

The nearest town was almost 60 miles northwest of the cabin, and Nicholas promised to be back in less than three hours. That was five hours ago. Oliver sat on the porch swing watching the sun leave, wondering if Nicholas left, too, again. To keep himself from yelling in anger, Oliver began making excuses for Nicholas' absence: maybe he got lost, or he got a flat tire. Anything is possible, Oliver thought as tears washed his cheeks.

"Is this happening to me again?" Oliver asked himself out loud.

As he gently swung, Oliver kept hearing what sounded like a phone ringing, but it sounded like it was in the distance, not getting closer. It took many rings, but eventually, Oliver recognized the faint sound. He jumped out of the swing and ran into the house, looking for the source. It was louder now that he was inside, but the cabin was big, and he had no idea where the phone could be. Oliver opened cabinets and flipped cushions, tearing through the place like a robber looking for anything of value. He stopped suddenly when the ringing stopped. Then Oliver spent another 20 minutes searching before finding a satellite phone tucked away in a kitchen drawer, almost hidden. It looked just like the one he came to hate at Redwood Manor.

Holding the phone tightly, Oliver sat on the floor with his back against the couch. He was hitting his head with his free hand, angry at himself for falling into the same trap again. Was he that stupid, he wondered, or did he love Nicholas so much that he was blind to the cloud of chaos that surrounded Nicholas? As he pondered those thoughts, the phone started ringing again. Startled, Oliver almost dropped the phone.

"Hello?" Oliver cried into the phone, trying to stay composed.

"I fucked up," Nicholas said.

"What the hell?" Oliver yelled.

"I got stopped on my way into town," Nicholas continued. "The officer said I was driving too fast. I wasn't. But that is not the point."

"You've got to be fucking kidding me?" Oliver said, annoyed.

"I am only allowed one call, so you are on a group call with me and Lawrence," Nicholas replied, ignoring Oliver's words. Nicholas did not have much time, and he needed Oliver to listen. "I did not want Lawrence to be the one to call you with this news. He is working to get me released tonight, if not by the morning, so please sit tight."

"Sit tight?" asked Oliver. "You scared the shit out of me. I am trapped, yet again, on one of your remote properties—alone. I am getting sick and tired of this crap."

"I understand the inconvenience, Oliver," Lawrence chimed in. "I have ordered some food supplies for you. They are on the way to you now. You should have them within the hour. In the meantime, I assure you that Nicholas will be back with you in less than 24 hours."

"You have 24 hours," Oliver yelled at them both. "I am exhausted and will not continue to live like this anymore; you promised we would not. I feel like a broken record, but if you are not here by breakfast, I will not be here when you return. This is your last chance, Nicholas."

Oliver hung up the phone before Nicholas or Lawrence could say another word. He threw the phone across the room, but it landed in a pile of cushions. Oliver wanted it to smash against a wall or the floor, an exclamation to his frustration. As the bulky phone settled into a cushion, Oliver realized it was new, meaning it could not have been in the cabin when Peter was alive. His first thought was to accuse Nicholas of lying again, but Oliver decided that someone else had been in the cabin if Nicholas was not lying. And suddenly, Oliver thought that they were not as safe in the cabin as Nicholas had promised.

Even though he was alone, Oliver began yelling at Nicholas, venting, directing his anger toward the man he thought he loved, who, once again, was not around to receive Oliver's words. Oliver was sure that Nicholas did not bring the satellite phone with them. It was too well hidden when it first rang to have been unpacked earlier that day. Oliver believed this meant Nicholas had been to the cabin recently, maybe quite often.

"Surely he would not be that stupid!" Oliver said out loud. "I swear, if he and Juan Diego had sex in this cabin, I am going to burn the fucking place to the ground."

Oliver knew Juan Diego was not there now. He left Juan Diego on the bottom of a lake, fish food, but that did not mean that he had not been at this cabin with Nicholas sometime in the recent past. Oliver started to cry again, but this time, his tears were not for his love for Nicholas but his hatred towards him for the continued lies.

His tears would have poured out for longer, but he was interrupted by the honking of a car horn. For a moment, Oliver panicked but then remembered that Lawrence was having food delivered. At that moment, he wondered why Nicholas did not just have food delivered. If he had, the two of them would be together in the cabin now, and Oliver would not be having wildly random thoughts of negativity towards Nicholas.

Oliver opened the door to see an old, beat-up pickup truck parked where their SUV once sat. The driver signaled for Oliver to come to her by flashing her headlights. Oliver walked off the porch and across the yard. The older woman sitting behind the faux diamond stud-covered steering wheel pointed to the back of her truck. He grabbed one with each hand and stepped away from the truck. The large woman sitting behind waved and drove away. She never got out of the truck and never asked Oliver his name. She never said a single word. She honked her horn as she pulled into the clearing and then honked again as she drove away. Oliver stood in the clearing, holding the surprisingly light bags longer than anticipated. He looked around to take in the vast emptiness that was suffocating him.

Oliver finally brought the bags inside and unpacked them. He was hungry. After eating some fruit, he decided he could not sit in the empty cabin, staring at the walls, listening to his breath and accusatory thoughts. He needed to be outside. He wished he was back in New York: a walk in Central Park would help clear his head. Instead of wallowing in self-pity, Oliver decided to explore the property. He hoped it would keep his mind busy.

In case it got dark before he returned to the cabin, Oliver walked off the porch and moved to the left, carrying a flashlight. He noticed a worn but somewhat clear path that led into a wooded area and decided to see where it led. He was swallowed by the trees, walking a hundred yards in almost total darkness from the dense forest; his flashlight was the only brightness on the path. Eventually, Oliver came to another opening where he noticed a small structure, not quite a cabin, but bigger than a chicken coup.

Chapter Twenty-Six

Oliver dropped the flashlight on the floor as the door closed behind him. The setting sun struggled to provide light through a single window to the otherwise dark space. Oliver wanted to scream as he looked at the three bodies in front of him, but instead he stood staring at the grey figures, stunned. There was a time not long ago when Oliver would have screamed and would have run away without looking back. But not now. He looked up to the ceiling and saw the thick, knotted ropes that suspended each body from a large beam. The frayed cord was wrapped around wrists, each tightly bound in pairs. The arms held the rest of the body dangling, toes pointing towards the blood-stained wood beneath them.

The three heads looked towards the floor, exhausted and lifeless. The person responsible for this scene meticulously created an elaborate, demented work of 3-D art, thought Oliver. He studied the muscular lines of each body, wondering how someone could defeat the three statues of David. There was no sign of any hair on the floor, but all three bodies looked as clear and smooth as a baby's bottom, three perfect specimens of alopecia areata.

"How the hell did…" Oliver started to ask himself out loud without finishing his thought.

"There is no way one person could have done this alone,' he continued to speak as if the dead bodies might provide him with some answers, might be listening.

Oliver could see that each chest had a large gash, the central point from which each man was drained of his blood. From the brutal stab near the heart of each, Oliver followed the dried red river down the chest and abdomen, around the penis, and then down both legs, covering their toes. Below each body was a large pool of dried blood.

Looking at the men, Oliver assumed they were young, certainly no older than himself, and each about six feet tall. The three of them could easily pass as the star quarterback with the amount of muscle wrapped by their clear, hairless skin, thought Oliver. The man in the middle was darker skinned, with a smooth milk chocolate coating. Oliver had to get closer to this one to see the large, motionless butterfly tattoo above his crotch. The bodies on the other side of the black man were white, not quite tanned, but as Oliver looked at their faces, he could see that one was Asian and the other Caucasian.

"This does not make any sense," Oliver said, trying to justify the scene before him.

Chapter Twenty-Seven

"Come on, Bobby," Jake said as he looked back past Steve to the city boy on his first hike.

"Shut up, Jake," Bobby yelled forward.

"Stop giving him a hard time, Jake," Steve said, joining the conversation. "This is not a race."

"No, but I would like to go to the cabin before dark," Jake said.

"Or what?" asked Steve, laughing. "We will get eaten by bears?"

"Don't joke about that shit," Bobby yelled as he felt himself trailing farther behind his roommates. "Whose idea was this anyway?"

Jake and Steve reached a clearing and waited for Bobby to catch up. It was the first time the three had been outside of Boston together since being assigned as roommates at BU. A biomedical engineer, an electrical engineer, and a mechanical engineer, the three met at freshman orientation. Four years later, living off campus together in North Brookline, the three seniors were taking one final adventure before graduating, before going their separate ways.

Bobby grew up in the Watts neighborhood of Los Angeles. He lived in Nickerson Gardens with his three siblings and mother. He never knew his dad. Bobby was at BU on a full scholarship as the first child in his family to attend college. He blossomed at BU, found his footing, and fit right in. He considered Jack and Steve to be his best friends.

Steve lived a very different life from Bobby before college. Steve grew up in Queens. His mother was a hairdresser, and his father was a plumber. He and his twin sister grew up living a lower-middle-class lifestyle. Steve had been a boy scout, played football, and enjoyed the title of homecoming king before leaving New York for the first time and landing at BU. He had gone home to visit his family each school break until this trip he, Jake, and Bobby were taking now.

Jake did not have any siblings. Nannies and housekeepers entertained him throughout his childhood while his surgeon mother and corporate lawyer father buried their dead marriage in their work. He grew up on the Upper West Side of Manhattan. By his teen years, Jake was spending more time in Greenwich Village trying to define himself. It was there where he met Juan Diego.

A young Juan Diego, cast aside by Nicholas during one of their many arguments, found himself sitting at a café enjoying a perfect Fall weather day when Jake sat down at the table beside him. Jake was starting his senior year of high school, his last year at home. By this time, he had almost accepted that he was gay. He had not yet said the words out loud to anyone other than the reflection in his bathroom mirror, but he felt this would be the year he came out.

* * * * *

Juan Diego noticed Jake almost immediately. He was a handsome young man who looked more mature than Juan Diego, cursed with his father's youthful, good looks. Juan Diego was still fuming over the argument he had with Nicholas.

"Bad day?" Jake asked Juan Diego.

"My boyfriend just broke up with me," Juan Diego lied. "And he kicked me out of his apartment, too."

"That is awful," Jake replied as he picked up his latte and moved to sit at the same table with Juan Diego. "May I?" he asked as he sat down.

Juan Diego signaled that it was okay, and they sat in the café and talked for hours. From the depth of their conversation, Jake assumed that Juan Diego was not much older than he. As Jake consoled his new friend, he admired Juan Diego's features.

"I've never had a boyfriend," Jake interjected.

"Stay away from boys," Juan Diego said, half joking as he put his hand on Jake's knee.

Jake had never been touched by a boy before. As Juan Diego's hand caressed Jake's knee, Jake felt his body tingling in a new way.

"I'll be right back," Jake said as he jumped up and ran to the bathroom, hiding his growing erection under a cloud of embarrassment.

Juan Diego knew what he was doing to this minor. He was angry with Nicholas, and when Juan Diego got angry, he would find a stranger to have sex with, kill, or both. Jake was the unfortunate victim. Jake returned to the table, still embarrassed but confident in the words he was preparing to say.

"My parents are not home," said Jake. "Would you like to come back to my place?"

Juan Diego stood up, grabbed Jake's hand gently, and said, "Lead the way."

That was four years ago.

Jake and Juan Diego kept in touch, something very out of character for Juan Diego. After he and Jake had sex in Jake's parents' bedroom that first day, Juan Diego decided he liked Jake, or at least having sex with the minor. As they snuggled in sheets that smelled like parental abandonment, Juan Diego felt pity for Jake. Juan Diego knew what it felt like to grow up in a family that did not respect or understand him, and he felt like Jake was suffering the same shame, so Juan Diego let Jake live.

The two did not see each other for months after that afternoon. Still, Juan Diego surprised Jake at his high school graduation, rewarding him with a night of drinking and wild sex in a luxury hotel room overlooking Central Park. Juan Diego showed up again a year later in Boston. Then, two weeks ago, Juan Diego invited Jake to a cabin in Vermont. Jake asked if he could bring his two best friends. Juan Diego thought the more, the merrier.

* * * * *

"We are almost there," Jake said to his friends as Bobby finally caught up to Jake and Steve.

"Where are we going again?" Bobby asked, out of breath.

"My friend has a cabin up here," Jake replied.

"Is this that mystery friend you always talk about," Steve asked.

"I don't talk about him all the time," Jake said, blushing. Jake had only slept with one other guy since losing his virginity to Juan

Diego. He had not dated anyone. He met a guy online, and they hooked up a few times, but nothing more. Jake had fallen in love with Juan Diego, or at least the idea of being with Juan Diego. No other man could compare.

"I hope this cabin has a shower," Bobby chimed in.

"Come one, guys," Jake continued. "We have another 3-4 miles and will be there."

The boys continued their hike and finally came to a clearing. They could see the cabin on the far side. Lights were on, and smoke was coming out of the chimney. Jake was excited to see Juan Diego again, excited for his friends to meet the man he loved.

Chapter Twenty-Eight

Standing so close to the bodies, Oliver could smell the decay, so he turned and ran out the door for fresh air. Hunched over, holding his knees, Oliver dry heaved a few times before spewing what little food he had in his stomach over the porch railing. After Oliver stopped vomiting, he wiped his mouth with his sleeve, sat on the porch's top step, and cried. He was exhausted from crying all the time. Oliver realized that he could not escape from the shadow of death no matter how hard he tried. He was beginning to believe that for as long as he was around Nicholas, he would be surrounded by death, swimming in blood.

After a few more minutes, Oliver stood and went back into the shack. He felt that he was more prepared this time and was ready to look beyond the horror to see if he could figure out who the people were or how they got here. Oliver opened the door and, this time propped it open with a chair he found inside. It was dark now, inside and out, and his flashlight provided little help as he tried to play detective.

He failed.

The shack was spotless except for the blood from the three men. The space was void of anything else, not even a cobweb. Oliver was stumped, and eventually, he gave up. Through his eyes, no evidence or information in the shack would help him figure anything out. He needed Nicholas. He needed better lighting. Oliver walked out of the shack, closed the door, and followed the trail back to the cabin. He was defeated and disgusted, ready to call it quits with Nicholas for good.

As he approached the cabin, Oliver heard soothing classical tunes. Looking up at the cabin, he saw that the inside lit up. He did not remember leaving any lights or music on when he left. Armed with only his flashlight, Oliver slowly climbed the steps of the front porch and then opened the front door quickly.

"Hey babe," Nicholas said with excitement in his voice. "Where have you been?"

"I thought..." Oliver started.

"I told you Lawrence would work a miracle for us," Nicholas interrupted. "The trigger-happy Sheriff pulled me over for a broken taillight and then thought I looked like some criminal on the loose. It was me in the picture that he showed Lawrence and me, but it was a bad picture, so Lawrence convinced the Sheriff I was not his guy and had to let me go. Lawrence dropped me off about 30 minutes ago."

Earlier, Oliver would have wanted to run to Nicholas and hug him, to be embraced, but as he stood in the doorway staring across the room at Nicholas, Oliver was not sure who he was looking at anymore. Listening to Nicholas tell his story, Oliver reaffirmed an earlier thought about always running, hiding if he was going to be with Nicholas, and he was not sure he could continue to play that game.

"I started making some dinner," Nicholas said, trying to lighten the mood and change the topic.

"Are you okay, babe?" he continued when he looked up to see Oliver almost in a trance.

"I am not sure I can do this anymore," Oliver said as he finally walked through the door and sat on the couch, dropping into the cushions like the world was pushing him down into them.

Nicholas did not ask what Oliver could not do. Instead, he walked over to the couch, sat beside Oliver, kissed him on the head, and held him tightly. Nicholas knew that Oliver did not need words right now. He just needed to feel loved, to feel safe.

"Did you know there was a shack just through the woods," Oliver finally asked without looking up at Nicholas. He was enjoying the strong arm holding him close to Nicholas' chest. Oliver was inhaling the sweet smell of Nicholas, trying to cover up the smell of death still lingering in his nostrils.

"Yes," Nicholas said. "It was there when Peter bought the place. I believe it was a sugar house or something many years ago. There are a lot of maple trees on the property. If I remember correctly, this place was once a huge producer of maple syrup back in the day."

"Well, it is not full of maple syrup now," Oliver replied through tears.

"Of course not," Nicholas said. "The maple farm shut down more than a decade ago."

"It is full of blood," Oliver fired back.

"WHAT?" Nicholas yelled unintentionally, pushing Oliver away as he stood up.

"I went for a walk and came upon the shack. When I went inside, I was greeted by three dead men."

"I did not kill them," Nicholas said, trying not to sound guilty while sounding very guilty.

"I did not say that you did," Oliver replied, annoyed at the sudden intensity of their conversation. "But someone did kill them and killed them brutally, ritually, even. It seems that death is all around us. It always will be. We are forever stuck in the shadow of death. I am tired of it and unsure how much more of this life I can take.

"I know, I sound like a broken record," Oliver continued. "But something has got to give."

Still standing over Oliver, Nicholas walked away to tend to the pizzas in the oven.

"Let's eat," Nicholas said, changing the subject again. "Then we can talk more about what you saw."

Oliver noticed how Nicholas was avoiding the topic, avoiding talking about the old sugar house. He thought it was an odd behavior for a man who just claimed his innocence.

"I cannot eat anything," Oliver replied. "I am exhausted. I am going to take a shower."

Nicholas watched Oliver leave the room, and he was momentarily angry with Oliver for skipping dinner. Nicholas wanted to talk with Oliver about what he thought they needed to do next and his plan to stay ahead of the police. He did not want to talk about the shack. Nicholas knew he was innocent. He believed that if dead bodies were in the shack, they had to be there because of Juan Diego. Nicholas knew that Juan Diego was the only other person who knew about this place, but he was not about to share that detail with Oliver. Not yet, anyway.

When Oliver came out of the shower, he found Nicholas in bed. Oliver was still wrapped in a towel. He looked at Nicholas, who looked back at Oliver with sultry eyes.

"Can we finish our conversation?" Nicholas asked.

"No," said Oliver as he dropped his towel on the floor and slipped his damp, naked body under the sheets. Nicholas turned off the nightstand light, grabbed Oliver, and pulled him close.

"Not tonight," Oliver said as he pushed Nicholas's hand from his leg and rolled away from Nicholas.

Chapter Twenty-Nine

"Where are you?" Calvin asked impatiently.

"I am stuck in friggin' traffic," Eddie replied as he honked the car horn and yelled profanity out his window. "I am almost there. Do you already have your luggage?"

"Yes," Calvin replied. "I am on the sidewalk, near where you usually pick me up."

"Okay," Eddie said. "I should be there in five minutes.

Eddie hung up the phone and continued to cuss out his window. He was excited to have Calvin home. Calvin, on the other hand, was not as enthusiastic. He had spent most of the last six months chasing shadows, and just when he thought he had solved his case, the tracks stopped, and the trail went cold. His case hit a brick wall. Calvin spent the better part of the last month scratching his head about what happened. He was frustrated and wanted to dig deeper, but his boss forced Calvin to take a break. He needed a break and to take some time away from the case to come back refreshed with a new perspective.

"Need a ride, handsome?" Eddie yelled out the window, looking at Calvin.

"No thanks, I am waiting for someone hotter to pick me up," Calvin fired back, laughing.

"Get in the car, you idiot," Eddie yelled.

"Where are my babies?" Calvin asked.

"They are at home," Eddie replied. "They were out for a walk when I left."

As the two drove back into the city, they talked shop. It was what they knew, what they did. Calvin and Eddie put everything into their jobs, and neither liked to rest until they solved their cases. Since they were both on significant cases simultaneously, and both pointed to possible serial killing, Calvin and Eddie found themselves talking more about their cases than their relationship lately.

"I hit a wall," Calvin said. "And I don't know how or why. I think I finally have a single suspect. One person who is the line that connects all my dots, but he is a ghost, a shadow. It fucking pisses me off."

"I know what you mean," Eddie said. "I feel the same way. My guy must be bouncing around the country or maybe has a day job that keeps him dormant for periods. It just does not make sense."

"Can we eat in tonight?" Calvin asked as they approached the Belmont. "I am tired. I want tonight to be about you and me and nothing else, but tomorrow, I want to share my notes and get your thoughts on my case."

"That is why I love you so much," Eddie replied. "I was thinking the same thing, and I want your thoughts on my case, too."

The two laughed as they left Eddie's car with Sal, the valet, and walked through the grand lobby of the Belmont, one of New York's finer "old money" buildings from the Gilded Age.

"It is good to be home," Calvin finally said. "Good to be back with you, my love." The two held hands as they entered the private elevator.

"You might think differently once you see the library," Eddie said as he squeezed Calvin's hand.

As they stepped out of the elevator, they were met by Princess and Barnaby, back from their walk and ready to receive some attention from their owners. Calvin dropped his suitcase to hug and scratch both dogs as they fought for his attention.

"Did you miss Daddy?" Calvin asked. The dogs responded by jumping on Calvin and licking his face. He was in heaven, but he calmed the dogs down so he could see the library.

Calvin knew that Eddie often turned the library into his private crime lab. It was not uncommon for Eddie to have rolling presentation boards covered with ideas, thoughts, and anything else that Eddie deemed relevant to a case, no matter how small the detail. Still, Calvin was unprepared for the monstrosity that had taken over the library.

"What the hell is all of this?" Calvin asked as he pushed both doors open. The large room was lined with bookshelves, each packed tight with a book collection that Eddie's great-great-grandfather began more than a century ago. Calvin loved the collection of books, possibly more than Eddie, but that might be because Calvin did not grow up enjoying such a vast collection of knowledge and entertainment. Calvin felt lucky when he could get one or two books from the mobile library that would drive through his poor neighborhood once a month when he was younger.

"I told you," Eddie started.

"No," Calvin interrupted. "You said a case had taken over the library. This must be so much more than a single case."

"Nope," Eddie said. "Thanks to the police departments across five states, I have been slowly creating a collage of images that I believe are all connected. I have not been able to connect all the dots yet, but I feel like I am getting close."

"Okay, forget about waiting until tomorrow. I want to hear all about it tonight," Calvin said. "But can we eat first? I am starving."

"In or out?" Eddie asked.

"Let's order in," Calvin replied. "I want to hear about your case. And then I want to tell you all about mine. I need your help."

Calvin took his suitcase to the bedroom to unpack while Eddie ordered Indian food from their favorite dive restaurant a few blocks away. Eddie did not ask Calvin what he wanted to eat. Eddie knew exactly what to order. They knew each other that well.

An hour later, their doorman delivered two brown bags filled with small plastic containers of Indian food. As usual, Eddie ordered too much, but he liked the leftovers. Calvin poured a Pinot that he had brought back from California, and the two lovers sat in the library, eating, drinking, and trying to solve their cases.

"So, you see here," Eddie continued. "All of the Vermont homicides appear unrelated, except when you look at them together. Add the dead Brits in New York who are on record as traveling through Vermont to or near all the places of confirmed murders."

"And you think this guy in the hoodie has something to do with it?" Calvin asked, pointing to a collection of grainy photos of a faceless man in a dark hoodie.

"No," Eddie said. "I think he has *everything* to do with it."

The two continued to read notes, examine photos, and ask each other questions while nibbling on their cold Indian food. By the third bottle of wine, Calvin rearranged photos across boards—cross-contaminating the crimes. As Eddie watched, he noticed that Calvin was putting select images in a timeline. When he was finished, he stepped back to look at his work of art.

"Holy fuck!" Eddie yelled, almost spilling his wine. "Do you see what I see?"

"Yes, but wait," Calvin says as he pulls a stack of photos from his briefcase. "I needed your help, but now that I look at this timeline, I think I just helped us both."

Calvin laid out a set of photos that meant nothing on their own, but as he laid out the order, weaving them through the timeline he made of Eddie's photographs, the men saw overlaps and, in some cases, gaps filled when the two timelines crossed.

"Holy fuck!" Eddie said again.

"Holy fuck is right," Calvin said.

The two men stepped back, and as they studied the dozens of photos forming a pattern, they noticed three men appearing multiple times: Oliver McPherson, Nicholas Lawson, and Juan Diego Santiago.

"This Nicholas character has managed to elude the police, escape capture, or be released almost as quickly as he is in custody," Eddie continued. "Each time, he has a solid alibi and a great lawyer. The various departments would never be able to make these connections." Eddie pointed to various photos.

"This one here," Eddie said, pointing to a photo of Oliver. "He is the boyfriend. Innocent and unaware of his boyfriend's thirst for blood, at least that is how it reads in all his interactions with the police."

"Well, this guy," Calvin says, pointing to a sketch of Juan Diego. 'This guy has recently been seen in the Bay Area, Denver, Chicago, and New York. And he has left his share of blood along the way. We got word that he was arrested here in New York, and get this, for harassing him." Calvin pointed to the picture of Oliver.

"A love triangle, maybe," Eddie questions.

"I don't know," Calvin continued. "But I am convinced that our cases are connected a lot. I was struggling to connect some dots and was hoping you could help, but I was not expecting us to solve it on my first night back.

"It's late. Let's sleep on it and look at it all with fresh eyes in the morning," Eddie said. "My brain hurts."

Chapter Thirty

Oliver and Nicholas ate breakfast in silence. After rejecting Nicholas last night, Oliver struggled with what he wanted to do next. He was mad at Nicholas for the continual hell that he was living. He felt beaten and battered, and he unfairly blamed it on Nicholas. Oliver was also angry at himself for getting sucked so far into Nicholas' world; for letting himself fall in love and be blind to what was happening around him. Redwood Manor should have been the last straw, Oliver thought to himself as he finished his breakfast.

"We need to talk about the sugar house," Oliver said.

"I am not sure what there is to say," Nicholas said. "Until I see this bloody scene with my own eyes, there is not much I can tell you."

"Let's go," Oliver said as he looked out the window over the kitchen sink. Nicholas looked at Oliver's back while Oliver, looking away, let a few more tears roll down his face.

Oliver led the way, but once they were face to face with the shack, Oliver stepped aside to let Nicholas go first. He wanted Nicholas to experience the overwhelming stench, blood, and nudity.

"I am not sure I am ready to see this again, "Oliver said as he let Nicholas walk past him.

"It cannot be that bad, can it?" Nicholas asked.

"Three naked men hung in the woods and drained of their blood," Oliver yelled. "Is that not bad enough for you?"

Nicholas did not answer. Instead, he walked up the steps, and as he opened the door, he was smacked in the face with the smell of decay. It was a familiar scent. Nicholas stepped into the light-filled room to see the three men hanging, lifeless, just as Oliver stated. Right away, Nicholas wanted to blame Juan Diego because he believed that was what Oliver wanted to hear, but more so because the scene felt familiar to Nicholas. He and Juan Diego had hung and killed some people when the two were still teenagers. As Nicholas scanned the room for any evidence to prove Juan Diego killed these boys, Nicholas remembered the first time he and Juan Diego created a similar work of art many years ago.

* * * * *

Nicholas and Juan Diego had just finished kayaking around Lake Watson. They were not the only campers enjoying early morning activities. As they silently glided across the lake, watching the early morning haze dance just above the water, they could see several runners as they would appear and then vanish, running along the edge of the lake. Nicholas and Juan Diego were surprised to see so many people this time of year.

They purposely camped on Lake Watson in late Fall because there were usually fewer if any, other campers. The campground was popular in the summer months, but only the serious, die-hard campers popped tents between Halloween and Easter. It was the Fall break of their senior year of high school. This trip was meant to be the start of their adult life together. At least, that is what Juan Diego envisioned when he planned the adventure.

After rowing on the lake, Juan Diego prepared eggs and bacon over the open fire at their campsite while Nicholas relaxed in a folding chair. On land, they could no longer see any of the runners. Neither recalled seeing any other tents when they hiked the five miles from their car to reach this isolated campsite two days earlier, but the lake swallowed more than 350 acres of land, making it difficult to know if they were truly alone. They preferred to be alone; well, Juan Diego did. When they were alone, Nicholas focused all his energy and attention on Juan Diego, but when they were in the civilized world, Nicholas would talk about Oliver a lot.

Two hikers who stumbled upon Juan Diego and Nicholas' camp interrupted breakfast.

"I told you I smelled bacon," one of them said to the other.

"Sorry," said the second. "Don't mind him. He can smell food from miles away."

Juan Diego and Nicholas looked at each other, then at their uninvited guests, confused as to why these two people felt compelled to interrupt their peaceful setting.

"No worries," said Nicholas.

"We'd offer you some, but this one ate it all," said Juan Diego, smiling as he pointed to Nicholas.

Juan Diego did offer their guests some coffee, and the four men sat around the breakfast fire, dressed for the cool morning air. Juan Diego played Twenty Questions, a detective trying to solve a crime while Nicholas sat quietly, enjoying the additional company.

"Where'd you come from? Where are you going? Do you have relatives nearby?" Juan Diego asked inquisitively. "Does anyone else know you are out here? How long have you been out here? Are you a couple?"

The questions were answered almost as fast as they were asked, which surprised Juan Diego. The two hikers, slightly older than Juan Diego and Nicholas, were enjoying the attention of their younger hosts. After a while, Juan Diego pulled out a bag of edibles, and the guests' faces lit up with excitement.

Nicholas was displeased that Juan Diego was willing to share the bag of brownies. Nicholas had baked them himself, so he knew how potent they were, how quickly even one small brownie could make you feel on top of the world.

"What are you doing?" Nicholas asked Juan Diego annoyingly.

"We've always talked about doing *it* with two people," Juan Diego whispered into Nicholas' ear as he excitedly bit Nicholas' lobe.

Nicholas was not sure what *it* was that Juan Diego was speaking about, but he saw how excited the hikers were when Juan Diego mentioned weed. As Nicholas studied the two hikers' faces and then looked back at Juan Diego, he believed that Juan Diego was planning an orgy in the woods. He and Juan Diego had sex outdoors before, but always just the two of them. Juan Diego often suggested that they should add some others to make it all that more exciting, but they never did. Suddenly, Nicholas realized today might be that day.

Soon after Juan Diego and Nicholas met, Nicholas was awestruck at Juan Diego's ability to get anyone to do almost anything, no matter how outlandish it might sound. Nicholas grew to learn that skill for himself, which came in handy many times over the years, but it was Juan Diego whom Nicholas credits as the master of the skill.

Juan Diego returned his attention to their guests and suggested a game of strip poker. Initially, their guests were hesitant, but they were much more receptive after each swallowed a brownie. Juan Diego assured them that the campground was quite vacant at that time of the year, and as the morning went on and the sun grew brighter, they might be a little cold, but they could put more logs on the open fire.

Nicholas headed into the woods to collect more wood while Juan Diego set up the game. When Nicholas emerged from the woods, the younger of their guests was kissing Juan Diego's neck while the other was peeing into the lake. Juan Diego looked up and into Nicholas' eyes as Nicholas approached. Juan Diego smiled, a grin Nicholas had seen before. Nicholas knew then that these two men would die before the day ended.

The game was fast-moving, and after 30 minutes, Nicholas was down to his boxers and t-shirt while their two guests were down to two socks for one and one sock and boxers for the other. Juan Diego had only lost his shirt. They continued to enjoy more brownies, and before the hour was up, their guests sat naked and passed out in the two folding chairs. Still almost wholly clothed, Juan Diego and Nicholas, in only his boxers now, sat on logs admiring their victims.

"I told you this would be easy," Juan Diego bragged to Nicholas as he ran his hand down Nicholas' bare chest.

"Now, what do we do with them?" Nicholas asked. "These lightweights ate most of the brownies."

"We kill them, of course," Juan Diego offered matter-of-factly as if that was his plan from the moment the hikers arrived. "I have an idea."

While Juan Diego tied some ropes over branches of a nearby tree, creating what looked like two nooses, Nicholas collected their guests' clothes. When Juan Diego was ready, he and Nicholas carried one man at a time over to the tree and tied his hands in the noose, then repeated the process with the other. Nicholas tore one of the hikers' shirts to create a gag for each.

Juan Diego and Nicholas pulled the ropes together so both guests were hanging from the tree. Their wrists were bound, and their bodies suspended beneath their arms. Their soles were two feet from the ground. Nicholas put some logs under the dangling feet of each man and piled their respective clothes on the logs.

Juan Diego lit the two fires, and then he and Nicholas pulled their folding chairs close and sat by their fire, admiring the two naked bodies slowly roasting. It took a little while for the fires to get hot enough to start burning the men's soles. That pain woke them from their edible slumber, and they both started swaying, trying to escape from the knots. They swung around as the two pendulums cried muffled screams. Juan Diego knew the fires would never get big enough to burn the bodies. The flames were just for his entertainment. This was when Nicholas began to see how savage Juan Diego could be and how brutal he got with his victims.

Juan Diego wrapped a sock around a stick and lit it like a torch, then used that torch to set the pubic hairs of both men on fire. One of the two men had a hairy chest, so Juan Diego lit that on fire, too. He enjoyed watching them scream into their gags as their bodies were scorched.

Turned on by the creation before him, Juan Diego jumped up, grabbed a large knife out of a bag, and jammed it into the chest of one of the men. He twisted the knife around before pulling it out quickly. The second man cried more as he watched the first one start to bleed out. Juan Diego rubbed his free hand all over the bloody chest, then pulled out his dick and started to jerk himself off, using the blood as a lubricant.

Nicholas could not believe what Juan Diego was doing. He should have been repulsed, but he was turned on as Juan Diego shot into the air, smearing his victim's blood all over himself. Nicholas got aroused, so he grabbed the knife from Juan Diego and stabbed the second man multiple times. He held the body as he jammed the knife in and out of the man's chest and abdomen, hugging the body so it would not swing around. Nicholas was covered with the stranger's blood.

Juan Diego pulled Nicholas close and kissed him. Covered in blood, the two collapsed in front of the two dying bodies and started making out. By the time Juan Diego and Nicholas had finished having sex, their guests were dead, drained of their blood.

* * * * *

"What do you think?" Oliver interrupted Nicholas' jaunt down memory lane. "What kind of sick person would do this to someone?"

"I know you do not want to hear this, Oliver," Nicholas said. "But I believe this is the work of Juan Diego.

"I don't know how he knew of this place or why he might have done this, but that is what I think. That means you are not safe; we are not safe here."

Oliver stood at the base of the steps, looking up towards the open door. He was not going back into the shack. Nicholas was standing in the doorway, looking down towards Oliver. Neither was willing to move, and Nicholas could see the anger in Oliver's eyes.

"I think it best if we just burn this building to the ground and get out of here today," Nicholas said. "It might be time to leave the country."

"I am not leaving the country," Oliver said. "And I am done running. If you want to run away, then you can leave me behind. I am done."

Oliver turned and started walking back towards the cabin. He was angry and began believing that loving Nicholas was not worth it anymore. He could find a new lover, a less chaotic lover, he felt sure. Oliver made it to the cabin before realizing Nicholas was not behind him. He screamed in frustration as Nicholas emerged from the woods.

"Sorry," Nicholas said. "You took off took quickly. I wanted to find a way to lock the shack until we decide what to do about it."

"Do about it?" Oliver asked, turning around to face Nicholas. "I'll tell you what we are going to do about it. We are going to call the police."

"What do you want to tell them?" Nicholas asked.

Oliver was silent. He was thinking about the situation, playing out scenarios in his head. He was not ready to tell Nicholas that he had killed Juan Diego, not yet, anyhow. He was hoping he might never have to tell that tale.

"Well?" Nicholas asked again.

"I don't know anymore," Oliver admitted. "I am so tired of death and the police and running."

"Are you tired of me?" Nicholas asked as he sat next to Oliver on the porch swing. "Please tell me that you are not tired of me. Wait, on second thought, don't say anything."

Oliver put his hand on Nicholas' knee.

"Does that mean you are not tired of me?" Nicholas asked. He knew he was being foolish, but he had loved Oliver so much, for so long, that he could not envision a life without him. He feared the next words out of Oliver's mouth would be swimming in rejection.

Chapter Thirty-One

It has been two weeks since Oliver discovered the three bodies in Vermont—two weeks since Nicholas blamed the murders on a dead man. Of course, Nicholas did not know he was blaming a dead man, but he did know that he was not the murderer this time and wanted to be sure Oliver believed him.

When they returned to New York, Nicholas went to craft a story with Lawrence, leaving Oliver alone in his apartment to contemplate what they saw in the sugar house. Nicholas was prepared to help Oliver understand what had happened and to convince Oliver to move away with him.

"Are we going to talk about Vermont?" Nicholas asked as he poured more red wine into his glass. Oliver was still nursing his first pour; Nicholas was on his third.

"What do you want to talk about?" Oliver asked. "Yet again, I found myself alone. Yet again, I had to deal with dead bodies. Yet again, Lawrence came to the rescue. What more is there to say at this point? It is all so rinse and repeat by now."

Before they left Vermont, Nicholas asked Lawrence to get involved, to call the police and handle the situation, like he always did. Lawrence lied to the police, telling them he was preparing to put the property on the market for one of his clients when he discovered the bodies. Fortunately for Nicholas, the property was in a Trust, protecting him from facing the police about any more dead bodies.

The Vermont State Police still had Nicholas' photo in many stations. They were still convinced that he, or someone who looked a lot like him, was responsible for the trail of blood that spread across the state like a wildfire out of control. Even before they finished collecting evidence from the shack, Lawrence could hear the mumblings of some officers blaming their mystery killer for these new deaths. Nicholas chuckled when Lawrence shared those stories with him, even though he did not like that the police were not letting go of the idea that Nicholas was their guy.

Neither Nicholas nor Lawrence knew that the Vermont police had begun working with the FBI. Agent Dalrymple was introduced to Detective Babson, who then introduced Agent Dalrymple to many other detectives, all trying to piece together what they believed to be a series of connected murders.

"I want to be sure we are okay: you and me," Nicholas said. "That is all that matters to me. You are my everything."

"If I mean that much to you, stop lying to me," Oliver yelled excitedly, almost spilling his wine. "I know you tell me half-truths. I am not stupid. You get quiet when you start holding back from telling me the whole story."

"I am sorry," Nicholas said.

"Stop apologizing," Oliver said. "We have been together for a long time. Why are we still together if you cannot trust me by now? And please do not fire back some quick answer you think I want to hear. You need to really think about your answer."

"Well," started Nicholas. "For starters, I love you."

"I said think about your answer," Oliver responded as he put his glass on the table. "I am going to bed."

Oliver left Nicholas in the living room to think about their relationship. As Nicholas sat alone, working through the bottle of wine he had just opened, he thought about the last time someone asked the same question.

* * * * *

"Do you love me?" Juan Diego asked Nicholas, holding him in his arms.

"I love us," Nicholas responded noncommittedly.

"That is not the same thing," Juan Diego replied, and you know it. "Why are you so afraid of commitment?"

"I'm not," Nicholas said.

"Then tell me you love me," Juan Diego said with loving authority.

"Do you love me?" Nicholas punted back.

"I absolutely, unconditionally love you," Juan Diego sang.

"Why?" Nicholas asked.

"How can you ask that question?" Juan Diego responded. "What do you mean, why?"

"I mean, why do you love me? What is it about me, specifically, that you love?" Nicholas asked.

"Well, for starters," Juan Diego said as he ran his fingers down Nicholas' chest. The two of them lay under the blankets in their tent, snuggling to keep their naked bodies warm. The tent stunk of sex.

"Do not say the sex," Nicholas interrupted him. "Sex is not love. I love sex, and that is different."

"I was going to say that I love how your face lights up when you are happy. I mean truly happy. There is an innocence about it." Juan Diego continued. "Your eyes get a brighter green if that is even possible. It's as if they are smiling with you. And your lips take over your face as the most genuine smile engulfs your face. Anyone looking at you who see that smile knows you are excited, truly delighted."

Nicholas tried to shrug off the compliment but blushed more than he anticipated.

"That is another thing," Juan Diego continued. "When you blush, there is something so innocent about how your whole body submits to the compliment humbly and bashfully."

"Stop. I get it. You love me," Nicholas said.

"More than you know," Juan Diego said. "And I know that sounds cliché, but my world lights up when I am around you. My battery is charged. My reason for living is reinvigorated."

"And your desire to kill grows exponentially," Nicholas said, trying to lighten the mood.

"My desire to kill has nothing to do with my love for you, my sweet Nick," Juan Diego sang as he kissed Nicholas on the cheek. "My desire to kill is driven by my wanting to be in control. My love for you is fueled by my desire to be controlled."

"That is a pile of bullshit," Nicholas said as he adjusted under the blanket. "You are the last person who likes to be controlled. You kill for the love of the sport. I think you like having me around to participate, but I certainly do not control you in life or under the sheets."

Nicholas started to tickle Juan Diego, who squirmed and gave in to the strong hands. He tried to tickle back, and the two rolled around on the air mattress that covered the entire floor of the tent. The tickling game led to another round of sex, their third that morning and the second since killing the two campers who hung from the tree a few yards away. Juan Diego could see the two bloody bodies dangling from the ropes. He watched them intently through the tent opening as Nicholas fucked him.

"Another thing I love about you," Juan Diego said as they finished. "Is the way you feel inside me."

"That is not love," Nicholas said before kissing him again.

"I did not say it was love. I said it is what I love *about* you," Juan Diego said. "And you still have not answered my question."

"What was your question?" Nicholas asked as he kissed Juan Diego's neck, knowing the question all too well.

Juan Diego pushed Nicholas off him, stood up, and walked out of the tent. He stood naked, surrounded by nature, isolated from the world, and screamed at the top of his lungs. The trees came to life as birds fled their resting spots, frightened by the sound. Juan Diego picked up a large stick, walked over to the dead campers, and began hitting their bodies like pinatas. He was hitting them harder and harder as if trying to rip them open and enjoy the contents that might spill out.

Nicholas watched Juan Diego from the comfort of the tent. The air was brisk. He did not want to get out from under the blankets and expose his nakedness to the cool air. Instead, he watched Juan Diego beat the campers' bodies, almost oblivious to the cold air.

After a few minutes of beating the bodies, never breaking any skin, Juan Diego dropped the stick before falling to the ground himself. He was crying now. His knees took the weight of his body as he cried. Nicholas knew then that he had to do something, so he put on some clothes and walked over to Juan Diego with a blanket.

"You need to get out of the cold," Nicholas said as he wrapped the blanket around Juan Diego.

"Do you love me?" Juan Diego asked again.

"I love us, and that is the best I can give you," Nicholas finally confessed. "I am not sure I can love anyone if you want to know the truth."

Juan Diego grabbed Nicholas' arms, tightening the grip around him, locking the blanket on him for warmth. He held Nicholas for longer than Nicholas wanted, mostly because he was getting cold. Nicholas felt Juan Diego's tears as they fell on his wrists.

"What's wrong?" Nicholas finally asked.

Juan Diego stood up, pushing Nicholas back. He threw the blanket on the ground and swung around. Nicholas could see the rage in Juan Diego's eyes as he tried not to get distracted by the naked, goose-bump-covered body before him. He had seen that rage before, but it was always directed toward their victims, never towards him.

"I cannot do this anymore," Juan Diego said. "I have loved you from the moment I watched you step off the bus all those years ago at camp. I knew then that I wanted to be with you, to spend the rest of my life with you and only you.

"Killing people is fun, and it is nice that we both get off on it, but it is you being in my life that completes me," Juan Diego continued. "I want you, and only you."

Nicholas took a step forward, and Juan Diego took one back. For the first time in his life, Juan Diego was afraid. He was scared that

Nicholas would never love him. He was worried that he would hurt Nicholas, maybe even kill Nicholas, if Nicholas rejected him.

Fearful that he might be losing Nicholas, Juan Diego returned to the tent, dressed, and walked into the woods.

"I'm going for a walk," Juan Diego said as Nicholas watched him vanish into the trees.

* * * * *

When Oliver woke, he reached across the empty bed and wondered why Nicholas was not beside him. He looked around the room for any sign that Nicholas had come to bed the night before. He had not.

Oliver walked out of the bedroom, hoping to see Nicholas sitting at the table, drinking tea in the kitchen, making breakfast, or even passed out on the couch from drinking too much wine. Instead, Oliver walked into an empty space. Nicholas was nowhere in the apartment.

He noticed the wine glasses still on the coffee table. Both were still filled with wine, just as when he left Nicholas the night before.

"Nicholas?" Oliver yelled to the room. No one responded.

Oliver sat down on the couch. It felt warm against his naked ass, and he smiled, thinking Nicholas had been sitting on the couch recently. There was no other explanation for warm cushions in his mind. He sat back, sinking into the comfort of the cushions, trying to bury himself in the warmth he believed was left for him by Nicholas, and he waited.

Thirty minutes had passed before Oliver started to think that maybe Nicholas had not made a tea and bagel run. After forty-five minutes, Oliver accepted the reality that Nicholas had left. He even started doubting that the warmth of the cushions was from Nicholas.

Feeling defeated, Oliver grabbed one of the glasses of wine. After emptying it, he put it down and emptied the second glass, then passed out, exhausted and upset. He was a lightweight when it came to drinking.

Hours later, Oliver woke to the honking and beeping of traffic, pulling him out of his dream and back to the reality of being alone again. Oliver was prepared to forgive Nicholas again when he woke earlier that morning. He was ready to talk about Vermont and maybe even tell Nicholas about Juan Diego. But now, as Oliver sat in his apartment alone, he thought maybe being with Nicholas was not what he was supposed to do with his life.

Oliver was heading to shower when he stopped to pick up his phone from the dining room table. He flipped through apps to see if he had any voicemails, emails, or texts from Nicholas or anyone. He had none. Oliver had forgotten about his camera app for the webcam still sitting on the coffee shop shelf. He meant to collect it after he killed Juan Diego. As he closed other apps on his phone, he saw the coffee shop fill his screen. Oliver watched for a few minutes as people came and went. It was mundane voyeurism until he saw the handsome Latin man walk through the doors.

Oliver fell into a dining room chair and looked to see if the feed he was seeing was live or prerecorded. He watched closely as the man moved through the shop, getting closer to the camera as he walked up to the counter.

"How the hell is he still alive?" Oliver asked no one as he watched a man, whom he believed to be Juan Diego, order a drink and sit down to read a newspaper.

Oliver screamed at the top of his lungs. First, Nicholas abandons him again, and now he believes Juan Diego is still alive. Determined to address the issue head-on, Oliver showered, dressed, and headed to the coffee shop to confront the man he thought he killed.

Chapter Thirty-Two

"Are you sure?" Eddie asked into the phone. "Okay, I will be right there."

"Babe, get dressed," Eddie yelled through the vast apartment. "The police found a body."

"What?" Calvin yelled from the bathroom, still drying himself off.

"You heard me," Eddie said. "My connection here in the city just called. She said they pulled a body from the Lake in Central Park."

"And?" Calvin asked, still not clear about the relevance.

"It could be connected to one of our cases," Eddie said as he entered the bedroom.

In the park, Detective Smith oversaw the extraction of Juan Diego's body from the Lake. Oliver's hope of Juan Diego sitting at the bottom until the fish finished him was ruined when Juan Diego's body resurfaced and bumped into a paddle boat filled with teenage girls. The girls flipped their boat when they jumped up and down, screaming. One of them almost drowned because she refused to grab hold of Juan Diego's body to keep her afloat.

When Calvin and Eddie reached the Lake, Detective Smith had Juan Diego's body on a gurney, waiting to show it to them before sending it to the lab. As Eddie talked with the detective, Calvin studied the body, looking at the photo on his phone. It looked a lot like his guy. He smiled.

"That is my man," Calvin said to Eddie and Detective Smith. "It has to be."

"Are you sure?" Eddie asked.

"Yes."

"What do you mean, your guy?" Detective Smith asked.

Calvin showed the detective the photo in his phone and filled her in on his theory. He told her details she did not need, but he was so invested in this case that he often shared more information than required to get others as excited and invested as him.

"That is an interesting theory," Detective Smith replied. "Let me run his prints through the system and see what comes back. I will call you later, Eddie, once I have more details. But I do appreciate you guys coming down. I thought this would help your case, Eddie, but at least it will help one of your cases."

"Funny story," Eddie said. "Last night, we discovered that our cases are most likely linked, so you might have helped me after all."

Back at their apartment, Eddie and Calvin continued to rummage through the photos and reports each had collected from the various police departments across the country. Both were still convinced that the photo timeline they created contained the answers they needed. They just were not yet asking the right questions.

An hour later, Detective Smith called Eddie to say she would email some files that she hoped he would find helpful to his case. She did not go into much detail on the phone except to say that the dead man from the Lake had not been dead for very long. Detective Smith said that she could not say much over the phone but that the files had all the answers.

"Holy crap!" Eddie yelled as he looked at the files in his inbox. "We got him!"

"What are you talking about?" Calvin asked.

Eddie printed out several pages from the files Detective Smith sent over and pinned them to the boards in the library.

"Do you see it now?" Eddie asked Calvin.

The photo Calvin had been sharing with everyone looked like the guy the police pulled from the Lake. And the guy removed from the Lake was Juan Diego. They knew this because he was booked and fingerprinted not long before he died.

"Your guy's name is Juan Diego Santiago, which you thought all along," Eddie continued. "And he was arrested in Oliver McPherson's apartment building. That clearly connects those two men, and we already have connections between Mr. McPherson and Nick Lawson."

"Okay, so where are you going with this, Eddie?" Calvin asked.

"We now know your guy, and we now know my guys, and we see where they intersect," Eddie continued. "So, if Juan Diego is dead, I gotta believe Nick Lawson killed him. We could get him to talk if we bring his boyfriend in again and share this new information. Maybe even get him to give Nick Lawson over to the police. We could solve both cases before you head back to California."

"Do we know where to find Mr. McPherson?" Calvin asked.

"I've got his address right here," Eddie said. "Let's pay him a visit."

Chapter Thirty-Three

"What the hell are you doing here?" Oliver yelled as he sat down at the table across from the man he believed to be Juan Diego.

Pedro looked up at Oliver with a confused look on his face.

"I'm sorry, but do I know you?" Pedro asked.

"Seriously?" Oliver spat back angrily.

"Yes," Pedro replied. "Am I supposed to know who you are?"

Oliver looked around and noticed that the coffee shop was bustling with activity. He did not want to cause a scene, but he could not believe that Juan Diego was playing dumb.

"I am done playing games, Juan Diego," Oliver started. "If you are this obsessed, then..."

"My name is not Juan Diego," Pedro interrupted. "You have me confused with my brother."

"Come again? Oliver asked in disbelief.

"Juan Diego is my brother," Pedro said. "He and I are two in a set of triplets. My name is Pedro."

"Are you pulling my leg?" Oliver asked, still confused.

Pedro pulled his phone out of his pocket and looked through his photos until he found a picture of him, Juan Diego, and Javier. It was a few years old, but anyone could see the picture and know Pedro was telling the truth.

"See?" Pedro asked as he showed Oliver the photo. "That is me on the right and Javier on the left. Juan Diego is the one in the middle."

Oliver returned the phone to Pedro and sat down. He looked at Pedro's face to see if he was telling the truth. He studied Pedro's details: his eyes and nose. He looked at how his mouth moved. Oliver was looking for anything to prove Pedro's story wrong. He couldn't find anything.

"I am so sorry, man," Oliver finally said.

"No worries," Pedro said. "We get confused for each other more often than you think."

"I can imagine," Oliver said.

"So, you know my brother, and by the tone of your first question, you have some beef with him."

"You could say that," Oliver replied. "He tried to get between me and my boyfriend."

"Yeah, well, that sounds like Juan Diego," Pedro said. "Are you dating Nick?"

"You know Nicholas?" Oliver asked back.

"No," Pedro said. "But Juan Diego talked about him a lot, almost too much. I guessed since that is the one name he mentioned more than any other."

"What happened between them?" Oliver asked.

"I couldn't tell you," Pedro said. "I know they met at summer camp, and I know that they spent many years together, but in what capacity and for what consistency, I could not say.

"Juan Diego is not one for long-term commitments of any kind, so the fact that he and Nick were together for as long as they were surprised the whole family," Pedro lied.

"Then, one day, some years ago, I learned they were not together. Juan Diego would not talk about it except to say that they were taking a break.

"When I saw my brother some months ago in San Francisco, he did not mention Nick, and I never asked."

"You saw him in San Francisco?" Oliver asked.

"Yes," Pedro said. "He was out there for some job or something. He was not very clear with me; he never was when it came to what he did with his time. If I were lucky, he would tell me about a lover, but that was about it. He led a fairly private life, at least private from his family."

"So, what brings you to New York?" Oliver continued with his flurry of questions, changing the topic. "San Francisco is a pretty place; almost a tough choice between there and here."

"I was ready for a change," Pedro said. "San Francisco was great for a couple of years. It helped me find myself, if that makes any sense, but then I was ready for more hustle and bustle—ready to get lost in a crowd."

"I get it," Oliver said. "I moved here from Greenwich for the same reason."

"That is cool. So, are you dating Nick now?" Pedro asked. "Do you guys ever see Juan Diego? I left him in San Francisco, but that nomad never stays in one place for long, so there is no telling where he is now."

Oliver knew precisely where Juan Diego was, or at least he hoped Juan Diego was still lying at the bottom of the Lake, being slowly eaten by whatever lived in that water. Oliver hoped that Juan Diego's body never resurfaced.

"If I am being honest, "Oliver started. "Your brother is obsessed with Nicholas and has been trying to break us up. He showed up at our front door in California recently and threatened me, and I know he has been haunting Nicholas for months if not years."

"Sadly, that sounds like Juan Diego," Pedro continued. "Sorry, man. I would intervene and tell him to stop, but he would not listen. He can be quite hard-headed."

"He is like a dog with a bone," Oliver said. "But I fear he might have won the battle of the boyfriends."

"What do you mean?" Pedro asked.

"Nicholas walked out on me last night," Oliver said. He knew he was lying, not about Nicholas leaving, but about losing to Juan Diego.

Pedro put his hand on Oliver's and offered his condolences. He knew what it felt like to be dumped. Oliver did not pull his hand away. He liked the comforting feeling it provided, even though he was a little freaked out that the cloned hand of the man he killed was now comforting him.

"Thanks," Oliver offered back. "Nicholas disappears a lot. I am hoping that this time is not the last. I am here now because part of me hoped that he was buying coffee for us. I live across the street."

"Nice," Pedro replied. "I arrived a couple of days ago and have been staying at a hostel down the street until I can figure out what I am going to do."

"A hostel?" Oliver asked. "I didn't even know there were any around here. Some of those places can be horrible. You can bathe at my place if you'd like a hot shower. I know we just met, but you seem like a nice guy, much nicer than your brother."

"That is very kind of you," Pedro said, thinking how karma was repaying him for helping Jacob when he first arrived in San Francisco. "I'd love a hot shower." He squeezed Oliver's hand tighter.

Chapter Thirty-Four

Pedro enjoyed the hot shower. He did not need one but took one to keep his story believable. While the water warmed, Pedro rummaged through Oliver's medicine cabinet but found nothing interesting. When Pedro stepped out of the shower, he dried himself, hung his towel on a rack, and slipped into the clean clothes that Oliver laid out for him.

"I appreciate you loaning me these clothes," Pedro said to Oliver as he emerged from the bedroom, still shaking his hair dry. "They fit perfectly."

"You are welcome," Oliver said. "Nothing beats a long, hot shower. Are you hungry? Would you like to stay for lunch?"

"Are you sure I am not being a bother?" Pedro asked. "You are too kind."

"Not at all," Oliver replied. "It is the least I can do." Oliver was secretly hoping this kindness was helping realign his moral compass. As mad as he was with Juan Diego, and as much as he wanted him out of his life, Oliver still had trouble accepting that he murdered Juan Diego in cold blood. Now, Oliver felt that helping Pedro was his way of quietly apologizing for killing Pedro's brother.

Pedro joined Oliver in the kitchen, and they made sandwiches together. Oliver liked how quickly Pedro made himself at home and how helpful Pedro was with making sandwiches. It was as if Pedro had been in this kitchen before. Pedro could have sat at the counter waiting to be served by his host, but instead, he jumped right in, helping in the way a good boyfriend would help, a lot like Nicholas did. This collaboration relaxed Oliver, comforted him, and for a moment, he wished that Nicholas was standing beside him, helping.

The two sat at the dining room table, enjoying their sandwiches and conversation. Oliver thought about Howard and Camilla, the last two people whose conversations flowed effortlessly. Pedro was forthcoming with information about his family and his relationship with Juan Diego, and he even went so far as to reveal some of his love stories and heartaches.

While Pedro was comfortable sharing how he lost his virginity, Oliver was not as forthcoming. He was still a little guarded.

"I am sorry," Oliver said, interrupting one of Pedro's stories. "But I cannot get over how much you look like Juan Diego. You even sound the same. It is frightening to think about it."

"It's okay, man," Pedro replied. "You should try being in the room with all three of us."

Oliver laughed nervously, still trying to decide if Pedro was being honest or if this was Juan Diego playing an elaborate game.

The rollercoaster of life and death Oliver rode with Nicholas was affecting Oliver now as he sat talking with Pedro, second-guessing Pedro's intentions, and his gut feelings. He wanted to be happy, to live in the moment and enjoy his time with the man who mirrored his first kill.

* * * * *

While Pedro and Oliver got to know one another, Nicholas was across town watching Oliver talk with a man whom Nicholas believed to be Juan Diego, thanks to the camera still in Oliver's living room. Without any sound, Nicholas could only fret about when Juan Diego and Oliver became such good friends. The body language between the two was warm and welcoming, like lifelong friends reuniting or a couple new in their relationship. Nicholas was furious. The man he loved was hanging out with the man who loved Nicholas equally as much.

Nicholas knew it was time to take action, so he called Lawrence.

"Hi Lawrence," Nicholas said into the receiver. "It's time. I need to be on a flight to Scotland tomorrow, and I think it is time to liquidate all the US properties. I am going to need the cash once I cross the pond."

"Sure thing," Lawrence said. "I think we can sell most of the properties over the next month. Redwood Manor will take longer since it is tied up with the insurance company, but you have one bank account tied up in the Trust that owns the Vermont property. We did not sign that over to Oliver, so you can access those funds anytime.

"Come by my office in the morning, and we can get everything sorted out. I will get Gretchen to make the flight arrangements."

"Thank you for everything," Nicholas said. "See you tomorrow."

Nichola hung up the phone, still watching the video screen on his tablet.

"But before I take off," he said to no one. "I need to see you one more time, Oliver."

He closed the tablet and called a cab.

* * * * *

"Lunch was delicious," Pedro said to Oliver. "Thank you."

"You are welcome," Oliver replied. "I appreciated the company and the conversation. If you are going to be in New York for a while, we should do this again."

"I am here for the foreseeable future," Pedro said. "And I am having a wonderful time talking with you."

The two moved the conversation from the dining room to the living room.

"It looks like someone had a good time recently," Pedro joked, pointing to the wine glasses and bottles on the coffee table. One bottle was still half full.

"It was supposed to be one," Oliver said. "At least the wine was good. Want some?"

"If you are offering," Pedro said. "It is five o'clock somewhere, right?" he asked, laughing.

Oliver grabbed two clean glasses from the kitchen and returned with them and another bottle of wine. They spent the next few hours talking about anything that came to mind. They moved from headlines to art history to sports and eventually to relationships again.

Oliver poured the last of the second bottle into Pedro's glass. Pedro watched the final few drops fall and ripple across the big gulp Oliver poured.

"The last drops," Pedro said, laughing. "If there is a shop around here, I can grab some more bottles and bring them back if that is okay with you."

"You don't need to do that," Oliver said. "I mean, unless you want to. I am enjoying talking with you. I feel like we could talk through the night and still have things to say."

"Please, man," Pedro pleaded. "I am having a really good time, and if you are up for it, I would love to go pick up a few more bottles, maybe eventually order some dinner and continue getting to know you. You are a pretty cool guy."

"Yeah, I am enjoying this too," Oliver said, blushing. "If you want more wine, a store is just around the corner."

Pedro put on his shoes, and then, as Oliver walked him to the door, he took a chance and kissed Oliver on the cheek before he turned and walked out the door.

"I will be right back," Pedro said as he walked down the hall towards the elevator. Armed with directions from Oliver, Pedro stepped into the elevator in search of wine. He looked back and saw Oliver watching him leave. They both waved.

Oliver touched his cheek once Pedro was gone. He was not sure how to react. He liked it but was not sure if he should. After all, he thought to himself, he was just kissed by the mirror of the man he killed recently. Even more problematic for Oliver to digest at that moment was that he liked both the kill and the kiss.

Chapter Thirty-Five

"We are here to see Mr. McPherson," Eddie said to the doorman as he and Calvin entered Oliver's building, flashing their badges. "Do not call him. Just tell us his apartment number. We need the element of surprise."

The doorman was not on duty the day Juan Diego had the police crawling the building looking for him. He only heard about the chaos from his coworkers, so he was not surprised by the two FBI agents standing before him making demands. Once he told Eddie and Calvin how to get to Oliver's apartment, he returned to playing solitaire on his computer.

As Eddie and Calvin entered one elevator, Pedro stepped out of another in search of wine. When Eddie and Calvin knocked on Oliver's door minutes later, Oliver rushed to the door expecting to see Pedro.

"That was fast," Oliver said as he opened the door.

"What?" Eddie asked.

"Sorry, I was expecting someone else," Oliver replied.

"Who were you expecting?" Calvin asked.

"I was, um, well, it is not any of your concern," Oliver responded, annoyed. "Sorry, but who are you, and how did you get into the building unannounced?"

"Mr. McPherson?" Eddie asked, ignoring Oliver's question.

"Yes."

"Great. I am Agent Dalrymple, and this is Agent Dunraven," Eddie said as he and Calvin pulled out their badges again. "We are with the FBI and would like to ask you a few questions."

"FBI?" Oliver asked, a little nervous that the agents were there to arrest him for the murder of Juan Diego.

"Yes, sir," Calvin said. "Can we please come in and ask you a few questions?"

"Um, yeah, sure," Oliver said, stumbling with the right words. He could feel the sweat forming on his neck.

Sitting in his living room, Eddie and Calvin scanned the apartment. Oliver closed the door and joined them on the couch.

"Did we interrupt anything?" Eddie asked, pointing to the pair of wine glasses.

"No," Oliver lied.

"Okay, great." Eddie continued. "So, you won't mind telling us about your relationship with Nick Lawson?"

"Nicholas?" Oliver asked. "What do you want to know about him?"

"Well," Calvin started. "For starters, do you know where he is right now?"

"No, I don't."

"When was the last time you spoke with him?" Eddie asked.

"It has been a couple of weeks," Oliver lied. "I don't remember, exactly."

"And what is your relationship with Mr. Lawson?" Calvin asked.

"That is a great question," Oliver said. "He is supposed to be my boyfriend, or at least I think that is what we both wanted. I honestly don't know anymore. He is not the best communicator."

Oliver was surprised at how forthcoming he was being with Eddie and Calvin. They were not like the local police officers that Oliver interacted with. Eddie and Calvin were patient and calm. They were inquisitive, not accusatory. Oliver liked how easy they made it for him to speak openly with them about Nicholas.

"What do you mean?" Eddie asked.

"I mean, he has secrets," Oliver said. "I know everyone has secrets, but his are bigger, seem bigger. We can go days or weeks, sometimes even longer, without talking. I don't always know where he goes or what he does, and when I ask, I get cryptic answers."

"Has Mr. Lawson ever mentioned the name Juan Diego Santiago to you?" Calvin asked.

Oliver felt his hands get clammy.

"We know Mr. Santiago came to see you," Eddie said. "We know that he was taken into custody and later released. We assume you know that much as well. We want to know if Mr. Lawson was here when Mr. Santiago came to see you?"

Oliver was not sure how to answer the question. He started fidgeting with his hands. His face and neck started to feel warmer as he became pale.

"Mr. McPherson, are you okay?" Calvin asked, noticing that Oliver was not looking well. Oliver did not respond.

"Mr. McPherson?" Eddie echoed.

Oliver's body went limp, and he fell off the couch, hitting the floor with a bang. Calvin ran to Oliver and started to put his medical school training to work.

"Call 9-1-1!" Calvin yelled to Eddie. "He is going into cardiac arrest."

Chapter Thirty-Six

Pedro walked out the front door of Oliver's building and turned right towards the store, following Oliver's directions. As he made his second right turn, he came face to face with Nicholas.

"Excuse me," Pedro said as he tried walking around Nicholas. Nicholas moved to block Pedro from passing.

"I am done making excuses for you," Nicholas fired back. "You need to leave Oliver alone; leave me alone."

Pedro looked at Nicholas. He stepped back, and Nicholas stepped forward, grabbing Pedro's wrist tightly, almost hurting him.

"What do you mean leave Oliver alone?" Pedro asked. "And who the hell are you?" Pedro knew it was Nicholas.

"Nice try," Nicholas replied. "I am done playing your games."

"I don't know what games you are referring to," Pedro said, trying to remain calm.

Nicholas looked into Pedro's eyes. They looked different; they seemed browner than he remembered. As Nicholas studied Pedro's eyes and face, he was struggling to remember if he ever connected with Juan Diego. He remembered how Juan Diego talked about his love for Nicholas, but as Nicholas stood, holding Pedro close, Nicholas felt nothing.

"I don't love you," Nicholas finally said. "I never did. I loved 'us' and what we did together; how well we did it. But after a while, it got to be too much; you got to be too much."

Pedro did not say anything.

"It stopped being fun; the killing stopped being fun," Nicholas continued. "The sexual energy and passionate lovemaking that followed was always great, but that was not enough to sustain us. You know that, right?"

Pedro continued to stay silent. He kept staring at Nicholas, speechless, as if he was struggling to find the right words for the moment.

"You are hurting me," Pedro finally said.

Nicholas looked at Pedro's wrist, grabbed the other wrist, and pushed Pedro against the building wall, both hands pinned to the brick above his head. Nicholas got closer to Pedro, so close that Pedro could feel Nicholas' breath on his face; he smelled the halitosis filling his nostrils.

"I don't care," Nicholas replied. "It is about time you felt the pain for a change."

The two stood in this locked position for a few minutes, each studying the other. Nicholas would yell profanity every few seconds, spewing his frustration with Juan Diego. Eventually, Nicholas started crying.

Pedro took that moment of weakness and pushed Nicholas back, only to spin the two around so that Pedro was now holding Nicholas's wrists, pinning him to the wall. Nicholas was taken aback.

"You are pathetic," Pedro said through gritted teeth. "And you are weak."

Nicholas tried to free himself from Pedro's grip, but Pedro was stronger. Pedro moved closer to Nicholas, their noses almost touching, and then he licked Nicholas' face before kissing Nicholas on the lips. The kiss was forceful, almost violent, as Pedro bit Nicholas' lip, tasting the warm blood. Nicholas struggled to free himself, and after a few seconds, Pedro pulled back. Nicholas could see his blood on Pedro's lips.

"What the fuck?" Nicholas yelled as he licked his lips to stop the bleeding.

"You were always too easy of a target, Nick," Pedro finally whispered. "When Juan Diego first told me about you, I did not think you were real. He never falls in love, or at least never stays in love. But with you, something was different. All he would do was talk about you, so I had to see what was so special about the untouchable Nicholas Lawson."

"What?" Nicholas spat out with some blood.

"At first, I was afraid that you would figure it out, discover that I was not him, that we swapped places periodically," Pedro continued. "But you never did. By then, you were so in love with Oliver, so blind to anything or anyone else."

"What are you talking about?" Nicholas asked, still struggling to free himself from Pedro's grip. "And why are you talking in the third person, JD?"

"I am not Juan Diego, you stupid fuck," Pedro yelled. "I am his brother Pedro. I have been playing you for a fool for years now. Sometimes you were with him, and sometimes you were with me. Not once did you ever figure it out. Hell, Juan Diego never figured it out."

"That is not possible," Nicholas said.

"Oh, but it is," Pedro said. "Tonight, you thought I was Juan Diego. That is how out of touch you are with this whole situation.

You are so delusional and in love with Oliver that you have become increasingly oblivious to what is right in front of you."

"That is not true," Nicholas cried.

"The last time we had sex," Pedro started again. "That afternoon in the cemetery with me and then again at your hotel, but with Juan Diego; do you remember that day? You fucked both of us and did not even know it. What does that say about you, Nick?"

Nicholas was trying to remember back to that time in London. He was trying to remember every encounter he and Juan Diego had over the last few years, going as far back as summer camp. The memories were blurring together; the timeline was jumbled in his head.

"You are just fucking with me," Nicholas said as tears rolled down his cheeks. "Just leave me alone, JD, and leave Oliver alone, too."

"You are right," Pedro said with a laugh. "I am fucking with you. And I am just getting started." Pedro loosened his grip on Nicholas's wrists, and when Nicholas did not try to retaliate, Pedro let go of Nicholas completely.

As Nicholas rubbed his wrists, Pedro pulled a knife out of his back pocket and stabbed Nicholas in the stomach. He pushed Nicholas back against the wall with his left hand and made multiple stabs in Nicholas's chest and abdomen with his right hand.

"Your boyfriend killed my brother," Pedro said. "I bet you did not even know that. And now I am returning the favor by killing you. I am going to buy some wine and go back upstairs. Then I will get Oliver to fall in love with me."

"No," Nicholas yelled, spitting up more blood.

"Oh yes," Pedro said. "And then the minute he falls in love with me, I will gut him alive, just like I am doing to you now.

Pedro pulled the knife out of Nicholas' stomach for the last time. Nicholas's body fell to the ground, and Pedro licked the blade to savor the taste of Nicholas' blood again. Pedro looked down at Nicholas. He was having trouble breathing, spitting more blood every few seconds, drooling it down his shirt.

"Try and save your boyfriend now," Pedro said as he turned and walked away.

Be sure to check out more adventures of
Nicholas & Oliver by John Paul:

The Garden of Death
Published 2022

For the Love of Death
Published 2023

www.ingramcontent.com/pod-product-compliance
Lightning Source LLC
LaVergne TN
LVHW012014060526
838201LV00061B/4304